ADVANCE PRAISE FOR
THE HUNDRED-YEAR FLOOD

Tee is in Prague. He is running away from memory. He is running toward myth. He is searching. In Prague, Tee meets an artist and the artist's wife. Before long, the three are drawn into a fateful series of events as Prague is laid bare by a flood that only comes every hundred years. This beautiful debut novel by Matthew Salesses is much like that flood—epic and devastating and full of natural majesty.

—Roxane Gay, author of *An Untamed State* and *Bad Feminist*

A filmic, fast-moving, disjunctive ride, *The Hundred-Year Flood* rollicks through an exquisitely constructed plot to arrive at a surprising destination. Matthew Salesses writes taut, intelligent, lyrical sentences. He is definitely a writer to watch, and *The Hundred-Year Flood* is the novel to read right this moment.

—Robert Boswell, author of *Tumbledown* and *The Heyday of the Insensitive Bastards*

The Hundred-Year Flood spins the gorgeous and devastating tale of Tee's quest to find his place in the world amidst the richly haunted landscape of Prague. This is a phenomenally engrossing novel, cast in prose that is at once searing and poetic, and Matthew Salesses is a once in a lifetime talent.

—Laura van den Berg, author of *The Isle of Youth* and *Find Me*

The Hundred-Year Flood is a beautiful, transporting novel that lays bare the heartbreak and loss of the world while never forgetting its magic. A dreamlike exploration of how the myths and stories we tell—and those that we choose to keep to ourselves—forge our identities, this book will swallow you whole.

—James Scott, author of *The Kept*

How artfully Matthew Salesses transports his reader between Prague and the States, past and present. I fell under the spell of his lovely novel as thoroughly as his protagonist, Tee, falls under the spell of Prague and, in particular, of one of its inhabitants. *The Hundred-Year Flood* is a vivid, cunning, compelling narrative about inheritance and forgiveness. A wonderful debut.

—Margot Livesey, author of *The Flight of Gemma Hardy*

In this spellbinding novel, Matthew Salesses artfully weaves an intricate tapestry, shifting effortlessly between time, place, and identity while exploring all three subjects in the process. He succeeds in transporting the reader to a ghost Prague—a timeless, kaleidoscopic city layered with wonder and devastating sorrow.

—Kenneth Calhoun, author of *Black Moon*

Matthew Salesses's elegant debut is at once both minimalist and expansive, atmospheric yet grounded in vivid, astonishing details. *The Hundred-Year Flood* captures life distilled to its purest, most potent form. I'll be thinking about this story for many years to come.

—Kirstin Chen, author of *Soy Sauce for Beginners*

The Hundred-Year Flood is a beautifully wrought novel about a young man who goes on a quest for self-discovery and finds himself in a city of legends, demons, and saints. Here, Tee struggles to reconcile his desire to belong with his desire to be free—his desire to be someone with his desire to be no one at all. This book is a deep, wonderful, and incredibly complex investigation into the necessary and fertile tension between resistance and submission, attraction and repulsion, and the need to create versus the need to annihilate. Poetic and dreamlike, aching with loss, and filled with the strange and enduring power of myth, *The Hundred-Year Flood* builds and builds until everything— the characters, their histories, their relationships and animosities, and even the city in which they live, are borne up, taken over, and forever changed by the inevitable and unpredictable tide of fate. This is an exquisite, unforgettable book about the extraordinary demands of identity and the transformative power of art and love.

—Catherine Chung, author of *Forgotten Country*

The Hundred-Year Flood is an incredible literary achievement. It's not often you find a novel that is capable of accomplishing such conceptual sophistication while maintaining the narrative force of compelling fiction. At times poetic and emotional, at times brutal and devastating, this intricate tale about identity, loss, love, and purpose is a force to be reckoned with and an absolute pleasure to read.

—Mario Alberto Zambrano, Author of *Loteria: A Novel (P.S.)*

The
HUNDRED
YEAR FLOOD

The

HUNDRED YEAR FLOOD

a novel

Matthew Salesses

Salesses

Text copyright © 2015 Matthew Salesses

Published by Little A, New York

www.apub.com

Amazon, the Amazon logo, and Little A are trademarks of Amazon.com, Inc., or its affiliates.

ISBN-13: 9781477829547 (hardcover)
ISBN-10: 1477829547 (hardcover)
ISBN-13: 9781477828373 (paperback)
ISBN-10: 1477828370 (paperback)

Cover design by Patrick Barry

Library of Congress Control Number: 2014959624

Printed in the United States of America

For my wife

We do not know what is happening to us, and that is precisely the thing that is happening to us—the fact of not knowing what is happening to us.

—José Ortega y Gasset, *Man and Crisis*

Later you look back and see one thing foretold by another. But when you're young, those are secrets; everything you know is secret from yourself.

—Jayne Anne Phillips, *Machine Dreams*

CHAPTER 1
MYTHS

I

Before his father came and flew him back to Massachusetts General Hospital in September of 2002, these are the things Tee learned in Prague:

1. If someone sneezes while you're talking, what you're saying is true.
2. If your nose is soft, you're lying.
3. If you cut an apple in half and see a star, it's good luck. If not, it's bad.
4. If you step in shit, it's good luck.
5. If you pour molten lead into water, you can tell the future from the form it makes.
6. If your hand itches, you'll get into a fight.
7. If your nose itches, you'll get beaten up.
8. If you pour something and it overflows, someone you know will get pregnant.
9. If you lift your feet for someone to sweep under them, you'll never marry.
10. "To cry at the wrong grave" means "to bark up the wrong tree."

11. Often the legends of Prague have to do with selling one's soul to the devil.
12. Half of Prague will be destroyed by fire, half by water.
13. When the Czech Republic is in its most desperate hour of need, a sleeping army under the hill Blaník will awaken and defeat its enemies.

Tee wrote this list during his first week in the hospital. He woke on a wet pillow, and he scrambled over the railing of his bed and fell to the floor. He pinched his nose shut. Water rushed over him, thick and brown. But he could breathe. He stood and rested the back of his hand on his pillow—he had cried in his sleep again. He smoothed down his dry hospital gown and went to the window. The river outside was the Charles, in Boston, not the Vltava, in Prague. He pressed a sheet of paper against the glass, blocking the view, and wrote until the words blurred. When a doctor knocked at the door, Tee touched the bandage around his head and told himself there was no flood, he was in Boston.

The doctor switched on the X-ray board, and they stared at the back of Tee's skull. Where Tee had been hit, the nerves had fused together in shock, and the skin had knotted and died until a surgeon had to cut it off. Tee knew who had attacked him, probably—a Czech with an American name, Rockefeller, someone Tee had called friend. Tee couldn't remember what exactly had happened. The impact had caused some rare brain damage. He couldn't tell dates or remember song lyrics.

"Are you listening?" the doctor asked.

Tee stood on one leg and the doctor tested his balance. The solidity of the floor shifted like weather. For the second time that day, Tee was back in Prague. He was running, naked, under the fireworks on New Year's Eve. The wind slapping his chest. People pushed and sang and embraced. Then the back of a glowing leg slipped through the crowd . . .

A woman walked out of Tee's hospital room. But no one had been inside except the doctor and Tee. Tee started forward, and his balance gave out. The doctor held him up, linking arms, and called for a nurse. The doctor said Tee had to *want* to recover. Tee had seen that leg—that calf—before. Where?

Later that month, Tee would transfer to a rehabilitation center, meant to reorient him to the world he'd never understood. He would stumble down the halls, searching for a ghost. He took to stopping other patients and prompting them with abstract nouns. They had to get used to every kind of bewilderment. "Love," he would say, hands trembling, and someone willing might answer, "What goes up comes down" or "If you give a mouse a cookie." "Regret," he would say, and someone might answer, "A wish for a perfect life" or "Aging." "Hate," he would say, and some would remember why they were there.

II

The day Tee decided to go to Prague, his girlfriend pulled him aside at a birthday party in Boston. The talk had turned to 9/11. "Stop acting so tragic," his girlfriend said in his ear. "For God's sake, others are suffering worse. Your uncle only killed himself. He didn't die in the towers." That was when Tee knew he couldn't stay in America. He downed his IPA and said, "Only?" Everyone was talking about death, but he had to keep quiet. He was filling a container inside of him. Into it, he put the things he couldn't say—about the seduction of forgetting. When his container was full, he would dump himself out in one dramatic move. A case in point: by the end of that week, he had broken up with his girlfriend and requested a leave of absence.

On the tram back to Boston College from the birthday party, Tee remembered a word his uncle used to like, *posturing*. Why had that come to him now? His friends were not posturing; was he? As a child he had thought of the word as a topographical feature. His uncle, the pilot, collected maps. There was one map his uncle liked best—a map of the wars in Eastern Europe. His uncle had called Prague a city of survivors, an older, less-posturing Paris. Tee used to point out Prague on globes before he knew what *posturing* meant, when he simply liked the sound of the word. He'd forgotten that. He could hear his uncle flattening the *r*, describing spires from above, the glow of roofs. He could feel his uncle toss him into the air, that first flight.

He chose Prague for its resistance. A city where, for thousands of years, private lives had withstood the oppression of empires. Both world wars, countless invasions. In the weeks before he left, Tee imagined hiding from the Secret Police, giving up his home to save his ideals. That was what he had to do: resist, move on, leave the familiar behind. It would be his first trip on his own, as he'd gone to college three miles from where he grew up. His first trip not counting his adoption. Prague might be the perfect place, after all: a city that valued anonymity, the desire to be no one and someone at once.

Tee arrived in Prague in late December 2001 and met the artist and the artist's wife at the turn of the New Year. It snowed that Eve, once in the morning and again in the afternoon. After a late lunch, Tee took the metro to the ruins of the original castle, Vyšehrad. He carried a bottle of beer in each pocket. He had paid twelve dollars for a monthly transit pass, a dollar per Pilsner Urquell. Water cost slightly more than beer, a fact he noted in his e-mails home. He didn't miss his friends, though—he wanted to be alone, free of expectations. He stepped out of the metro station and into the wind at the top of the hill. A hundred feet down the path, the walls stretched along either side, keeping out a long-gone foe. At the far end, the Vltava ran below, a dozen feet lower than it would reach in August.

Tee bent his head to an arrow slit, shrinking the world into a guardable space. He imagined an army advancing, simply for something in their sparse world to take. Or maybe to take something back. He imagined a little piece of himself, held captive. He had been in Prague for five snowy days. The sun never came out. He wondered again if he should have gone elsewhere for his semester off. He'd enrolled in a certification course to teach English as a foreign language, but he was already skipping. What if the Czech kids saw his Korean half and had to know where he *came from*? Anywhere he went he was the only Asian in Prague.

The wind blew at his back. At the far end of the castle grounds, behind the Basilica of St. Peter and St. Paul where the devil had lost a legendary bet for a soul, Tee stood for a while in a famous cemetery. He watched a boy return to the same statue over and over, a thin, winged girl that couldn't have meant anything to him. Tee stepped back to give the boy room, or to wonder unobserved. After the boy's father led him away, Tee touched the wings. They were scaly, almost reptilian. He imagined the boy lifting those wings onto his own back. Making a myth of himself. Later Tee would learn about Queen Libuše, who sent out a white horse from Vyšehrad to look for a king and found a man stooping under a doorframe that would eventually become Kafka's castle. After that king died, a maidens' army would fight the men for control of Prague. Beside the cemetery was a prayer maze where children knelt in the center and wished. Tee felt cold with history. He poked a finger in the snow and outlined a man and a woman, a baby slipping out of their arms.

He climbed up and sat on the wall under the flat-bottomed clouds. Below, ancient armies had piled up dead, forever at the edge of what they wanted.

Then Tee was back at his uncle's wake. His uncle, burned up from crashing his solo plane in a wheat field in New York, had been cremated and kept in a teal urn. Tee's aunt shrieked with guilt, pressed her forehead to the ceramic. His father buried his face in his shirt. They could no longer hide their affair. The two of them had driven the plane down as effectively as had his uncle's hands. Yet the affair was many years old. Why had his uncle given up at last?

A piece of brick scratched free under Tee's nails and tumbled toward the water.

He wandered down the hill, through an arch in the wall. A flash of color in the dark: a picture of fireworks and, underneath, in English, NEW YEAR EVE. In a day, Tee reminded himself, it would be 2002. Other announcements lay scattered on the cobblestone, all in Czech. He wondered why this single English flyer was left on the wall. The type of everyday strangeness that thrived in Prague. He folded the flyer into his pocket.

When he reached the city center, it was dark but not late. Winter curtained Prague at four in the afternoon—so cold sometimes it was like the city was searching out the gaps in his clothing. Though other times he would stumble upon a hidden garden, as if pumped through the arteries of a secret heart.

In his pocket, his fingers found a tiny piece of scaled wing. At some point he had started taking "souvenirs" from the places he went, coasters he doodled on, a loose chunk of brick, severed buttons. He remembered lying in bed after the birthday party in Boston, a candle in his hand, wondering why he had taken it—the number 2. Later, on his first day at the artist's house, he would steal a pewter Golem, just bigger than a Monopoly piece.

He needed coffee. He needed to believe his exhaustion was only jet lag, though he had woken on the cold floor that morning, as his father would do sometimes. He had slept late despite the rooster that crowed periodically, a rooster in a city in winter. He heard its pecking in his head—*shush, shush, shush*—its beak slicing vainly through the snow.

In a café down a side street, he let the caffeine wind his spring. He wondered how to make a start: apply at the *Prague Post* (the local English newspaper); work at an English bookstore; commit to teaching, after all; write a novel; become a tea connoisseur? As if one of those tasks would open a door. It wasn't about work. After his uncle's air limo business sold, Tee's share of the inheritance (a token for a son-like nephew) would be nearly three hundred thousand dollars.

By ten, he had finished his third cup. He trembled as he signed the check. In the dark, on the cobblestone, he didn't know which way to turn. He smelled smoke, heard a siren somewhere. His heart raced. After an hour he stumbled upon the familiar glass doors of his hotel, as if by coincidence. No one waited inside. He remembered skimming over Boston in the cockpit of his uncle's water plane, so completely separate from the city below. In the glass doors stood his reflection. The container inside of him filling. Finally he made his way through the web of streets to a beer stall near Old Town Square. As he waited for his Budvar, he heard the explosions, at last. He followed a woman a little older than he. When they reached the crowd, he saw the fireworks. Not high up in the air, but shot horizontally down streets, just overhead. He pushed through the mob under the Orloj astronomical clock, under the streaks that burst into sparks and ash. Inside his coat pocket, his fist tightened on the scaly feather. A stranger slapped his back. The Orloj rang in the New Year with its famous dance of figurines. People sprayed champagne, shook hands, passed bottles, sang Czech folk songs, pulled him into crisscrossing arms. He drank anything he got his hands on. A liquor that tasted like Christmas, which he would later know as Becherovka. A jam jar of homemade slivovice. The champagne wet his clothes, stuck to his skin, and suddenly he wanted everything off. He felt dizzy with the idea of starting out clean of his past, like a baby. Dumping his container for good.

He slipped off his shirt and stepped into a small opening where two businessmen shot industrial-grade fireworks over Týn Church. When he got down to socks and boxers, the crowd cheered him, the foreigner half-naked. He swayed and shuffled to the side to catch his balance. Someone copied his steps, making a dance. Someone handed him another Budvar. He wriggled, trying to force the heat from the alcohol through his limbs. The wind stung his back. He drank and shook and drank and shook—until finally the cheers faded. As if, in the end, he was only odd or sad. People returned to their circles. Hands drew back. Tee shook harder. The glass bottle steamed in his palm. As he kicked off his socks, a couple approached, a shabby-looking man and a much taller, graceful woman, and waved him over. The man pulled a hood over shaggy hair and ducked under a Roman candle. The woman pointed at the sky and caught Tee's gaze. He was going to cry, but why? When he had gathered his clothes, the woman turned to him with dizzyingly blue eyes and asked if he spoke English. "We think you should be painted," she said with no introduction or self-consciousness. Tee picked up a fallen piece of a rocket, as if it still had the energy for another burst. He added it to his pile of clothes, dusting them with ash, and followed her.

III

The artist went by the nickname Pavel Picasso. He had become famous during the Velvet Revolution in 1989, when Prague intellectuals had led a nonviolent revolt against the Communists. His art, as one critic had slyly put it, punning on "Communism with a human face," excelled at a "faceless humanism." Pavel Picasso was a man of average height, average build, but rare intensity. It seemed to Tee as if some inner measure pulled the outer reaches of the artist's body and personality toward a central point. Sometimes paint stained Pavel's mouth as if it started inside him. He chewed his knuckles as he worked. He thought with his hands in his armpits. Tee would spend much of January and February of 2002 posing in the studio in the artist's bedroom, trying to be worthy of intensity.

While Pavel painted, his wife, Katka, would tell legends like that of the Devil's Pillar, dropped by the devil through the roof of the basilica in Vyšehrad. She would wave her hand as if to call the past onto stage. She was a tall woman, never awkward about her height, with brown hair to her shoulders and high, round cheekbones. She could sweep out her arms and take over the room. When she wasn't talking, she brewed tea, cooked breakfast and lunch. But domesticity didn't seem natural to her.

Tee would move to help her, and Pavel would peer down his cigarette and tell him to hold his pose. "Now try to being more American," Pavel would say. It was nerve-racking to Tee, being objectified by an artist's gaze—he was used to being an object of dismissal. He tightened his jaw. Sweat under his chin.

Early in the morning before Tee's first visit to the artist's house, he stood in front of his bathroom mirror for longer than usual, wondering what Pavel Picasso would see. As soon as Tee turned away from his reflection, he would forget it. He knew this.

Katka had sketched a map to Malešice on his palm. When he arrived at the house, she led him into the bedroom, where light pooled through two high windows. She walked quickly on her tall frame, and he had to hurry to keep up, even for those few steps. He didn't want them to think he had stopped to examine their lives. On their walls hung completed puzzles, elegantly framed, not paintings. There was a photo from their wedding: only their shaggy hairstyles seemed to have aged. He was surprised at how ordinary the couple seemed, sober and without fireworks. Katka pointed to a chair across from where Pavel was setting up, and Tee sat with his head in his hands, then straightened up so that they wouldn't think he was having second thoughts.

Katka knelt and looked directly into his eyes. That blue was hypnotic, the inner blue of fire. "Where in America did you leave?" He was glad, at least, that she asked *leave*, that she believed in his dispossession. And who else, when he had stripped all the way down, had wanted to make something of him?

"You're not expecting me to undress again?" he asked, blushing.

She pointed to his hand. "You could have copied the map." He hadn't thought of that. If he had erased the route on his skin, he might not have come.

- - -

The first, and best, painting of Tee depicted a dark figure rising off his toes beside the Orloj, a ghost learning to let go of the earth. Below his black bangs, Tee's cheeks burned red with faith. He had never seen in himself this odd credulity. The recognition stuck in his throat, scratching as he breathed. He wondered if his Korean half—some moment during his first months of life, after his birth mother's death but before adoption—was responsible. He remembered a piece of family lore about how he had learned to walk. He had refused to crawl, only stood until his legs held up his will. His mother had said it was like watching someone recall who he was. Katka said Pavel painted more real than life.

By the end of his first week, Katka had given Tee a short version of her own history, how she had run off from her mother and her small town, Beroun, in 1984, to go to university in Prague. She spoke English with a slight British accent, inherited from her late father; behind the rising intonation was her mother's guttural Czech. Hard consonants, throated vowels, rolled, nearly hiccuped *r*'s—Tee found the combination exciting, like a car race in which one watches to see how the next crash might unfold. "I wanted a new life then," she said. "Heaps of us did." She reached over and readjusted his pose, and he realized that she and her husband somehow worked together, though only Pavel held a brush. Her confidence was different than Pavel's—it wasn't based on a talent. It was more mysterious, like the faith in Tee's cheeks.

That first week, Katka told a legend about the Orloj's maker, Hanuš. Upon the clock's completion, an executioner blinded him with a hot poker. "The city's orders," Katka said, "so that he could never make another." She smiled, and turned her wrist as if to bore Tee through each eye. "Then the story splits in two. At some point the clock broke. Some say Hanuš took revenge. He threw himself into the gears. Others say the clock broke on its own, and no one but Hanuš could fix it. He fixed what he had got blinded for making."

"Either way," Tee said, "that's a man who knew what could live forever."

Pavel snapped his fingers. "Stop moving."

For a moment Tee had nearly forgotten he was being painted.

"Tell me," Katka said, "do you know a book called *The Giving Tree*?" She folded her hands.

"Are you asking because it can help Pavel paint me?"

"She asking anyone who's speaking English," Pavel said.

Katka explained that *The Giving Tree* had been her father's favorite book to read to her. Tee knew it. The tree gives up its apples, its branches, its trunk, for a boy.

"I always thought that story was so beautiful, but my dad read it like a warning. Later, he killed himself." There was a long pause. "What were you like as a kid?"

Tee rubbed his eyebrow and marveled that she could mention suicide so easily. Was that when she had left for Prague? They might understand each other. "Most of the time, I did what I was told. Then all of a sudden, I would break a window or run away."

He asked if she believed in her legends, and she shrugged. Then she tousled his hair. "You are too young for these old stories to interest you." She and Pavel were fifteen years his senior. Tee wondered again why they had chosen him to model.

Once, about a week into their sessions, she said, "Are you ready to say why you came here yet? Was it because of the terror attacks? You seem like you have got some dark past."

"I came here," Tee started—but then he didn't want to look like a kid sighing about his uncle—"because here my past doesn't matter."

He wished to explain better. Prague had resisted centuries of violence with a peaceful revolution. He tried again. "I came here because here I'm the only one who determines who I am." Why did that sound like *finding himself*? He wasn't wasting his uncle's money, or affection. His container grew fuller. With a start, he couldn't remember if he had undressed, after all. He glanced down, though, of course, he was clothed.

"You look like you saw a ghost," Katka said.

Pavel reminded him, once again, to keep still.

Each day, as his body came to life on the canvas, Tee would wait to hear about Katka's and Pavel's pasts, and the city's. His own past he avoided—nothing about him seemed equal to either of them. His accomplishments were Most Sportsmanlike at soccer camp, two years on the school newspaper, one TV appearance to give his reaction to a series of campus robberies, the ability to drink a beer faster than anyone else in his book club. Pavel and Katka would never have seemed equal to each other without art. Her length and self-assurance; his tics and self-containment, always curled up, seeming smaller than he was. At times, Tee wasn't sure if it was the stories or being painted that he liked more. Her crashing voice kept him still and rapt. But taking shape, as the artist saw him, Tee almost felt he had a purpose in Prague.

It wasn't long, though, before Pavel handed over an old painting as a thank-you and said Tee didn't have to come anymore. Katka leaned forward. Tee smelled cocoa butter, noticed her lipstick printed on her cup. He wanted to rub a piece of paper over the print. How long did it take to finish a painting? Surely years, or at least months.

"What is it?" Katka asked, squinting.

It was just as she had said. In the paintings, he was more real than life. His original self had been replaced. He pointed to her cheek. "You have something there." She ran her finger along her nose, and without thinking, he licked his thumb and pressed it to her skin. He lifted off an eyelash. Before he could pull away, she held his wrist and blew on his thumb.

Pavel stomped, and his brown hair flopped over his craggy brows. He puffed it aside. He said these were the last touches and Tee should shut his eyes if he couldn't stop.

Tee felt like a child, but he did shut them. With his eyes closed, he realized how tired he was. Though he'd done nothing all day but pose. He heard Katka start a new legend, about the hill Blaník, as if nothing had changed, at least for her. In the darkness, he became terrified of losing them, of losing that gaze on him and the stories that contextualized the city. He didn't realize yet how much he needed them to contextualize him. He squeezed his eyelids tighter and the room expanded and then contracted. He pictured his father with a camcorder, taking one of his home videos: Pavel Picasso painting furiously, Katka narrating some deeper mystery, Tee a stranger in a strange land. His father, who had slept with his aunt. That had nothing to do with Tee. Heat pressed his thigh, and he opened his eyes. His leg was touching Katka's. She put a hand on his knee, to reassure him or to question his alarm.

"Close eyes," Pavel said again.

Tee didn't make any move until Katka's palm lifted. When he had broken up with his ex in Boston, she had said he was the same as his father. "You will only ever want the wrong woman," she'd said, meaning she should have known they weren't right for each other.

Katka stood and went to her husband's side. She hummed some Czech tune, and Pavel's frown faded.

After lunch, Pavel again tried to hand over the thank-you painting. "Why stop now?" Tee said. "You could do a bigger series. You could try a gallery in New York." Without the sessions, Tee might simply return to New Year's, trying and failing to explode. Pavel clamped his hands in his armpits and said Tee's suggestion was what his closest friend, a Czech with an American name, Rockefeller, had been advising for years.

Katka turned Tee gently by the shoulder. "Wait a second. Do you mind?" she asked. He hesitated, then stepped outside beside the big maple tree dusted with snow. He walked around it several times, until he lost count. He made a snowball, but had no target. His hands grew numb. Finally he held the snow to his face, the cold waking him up.

When Katka called him back, the smell inside the kitchen still thick with meat and cabbage, she said he could return tomorrow. She pulled apart a knot in her hair and grimaced. He didn't know who had wanted him and who hadn't.

That night, he lay in bed picturing Pavel's hands curled into claws. *Could*, Katka had said, not *should*. Though she was speaking her second language. Tee hadn't even looked at the thank-you painting. He didn't know what exactly Pavel had been trying to give him. Maybe it wasn't a painting but one of the puzzles Katka had hung around the house. Tee was intrigued by her puzzle-making, the things about her that didn't make sense with her legends. Once every other week, she went to the cinema, but she only watched documentaries. She looked up the story beforehand. She wasn't interested in the mystery of what happened but in its representation, in how it was put together by someone else.

After that *could*, Pavel had said the subject should choose the next pose—that was why Tee couldn't sleep now. He had thought this was a serious request. He had spread his fingers across his chest, and then he hadn't known what to do with his other hand. He hadn't known whether to sit or to stand. He held his palm stiffly over his heart, as if to pledge allegiance. For the first time, he heard Pavel laugh. When Tee woke, he couldn't find pants to match his shirt, though he had worn that shirt a dozen times and had laid out an outfit the night before.

- - -

On days Pavel was happy with his work, he would join them in telling legends. His accent was like a Shakespearean character's, iambic, weighted with beats. He liked to talk about a famous Czech hero, Jára Cimrman, who had never actually existed. "So Cimrman crossed ocean in a steamboat," he would say. Or "So Cimrman took submarine to moon." Cimrman had climbed the Andes, braved the Arctic, suggested the Panama Canal but never got the credit. Katka teased these stories out of him, laughing, but Tee didn't get the joke.

Tee wished they would tell him more about life under Communism. Whenever the subject came up, his hip twinged as if he might walk, by accident, into a decades-old rally. One afternoon a small group protested a former Communist prime minister's acquittal. Pavel and Katka went with their friend with the American name, Rockefeller. The next morning, when Katka described how Pavel had seemed ready to smash a painting over a policeman's head, Tee made his way across the room. "What was it like?" he demanded, "the Revolution?" He imagined falling in love over art, brushstrokes inciting a nation to freedom, Pavel's paintings hanging on the facade of the museum in Wenceslas Square, an idealist burning himself beneath.

Pavel sighed and traded brush for cigarette. "It was like something, history, could never being stopped."

Tee felt his armpits sweat, a change in circulation. "I want to understand," he said. "There was so much against you. You must have had a lot of conviction." His elbow bumped the easel. He ignored the shiver up his arm.

Pavel steadied the canvas. "Impossible to understand," he said. "When I'm eleven, I saw boys I knew once try to kill a man in alley. They are taking nothing, only putting knife in him and running. Maybe he is living, maybe not. I didn't know they Secret Police or he was, maybe no one."

"What did you do?" Tee asked.

"I ran away."

"We all did what we had to do," Katka said. "You lived. You survived."

Pavel blew thin darts of smoke, one after another.

Tee wanted more. Maybe he could offer a story of his own. His uncle had suddenly committed suicide after putting up with an affair for more than twenty years. A story with no moral and unclear conviction. What would they make of that? But then Katka rested her hand on the back of her husband's neck, and Pavel went on. He talked about the political art that got his father killed, about his own paintings denouncing Communism, about how Rockefeller and Katka had placed his art around the city. They had been a family, the three of them.

"Is different than you think," Pavel said. He said that Tee reminded him of how they used to "risk self" to print their samizdats. They had risked more than Tee ever would.

"I'm painting boy here," Pavel said, "who is holding door for somebody and then forgets and closes it. But the somebody behind of you is you."

"You painted me holding a door for myself?" Tee tried to translate Pavel's English. "And then shutting it on myself?" He pictured coming upon a door like the glass doors of his hotel. He sensed a person behind him, so he held it open. Yet after a moment, he gave up and stepped inside.

Of course, it was a paradox. He couldn't hold the door for himself and still enter. He remembered an afternoon in Old Town Square, a man in a parrot suit. "Thai massage," the parrot yelled, approaching him. "You Thai. This your massage." For a moment the parrot and the door combined. Maybe Tee could only ever belong to Prague as a foreigner, as the one Asian in the entire city, someone with another self waiting in the wings.

But that lesson, as Pavel had said, Tee would soon forget.

Katka seemed to study Tee with the same critical eye as her husband's. Heat radiated off their bodies. Tee felt her heat separate from Pavel's, or maybe that was an illusion. He waited for more explanation, for some final clarity. He waited for an explanation of their beautiful revolution. He wanted to know how they had risked so much. But instead, Pavel described the first time the Secret Police took his father, in 1978, a story Tee would always remember, always imagine, as a moment of definitive loss.

IV

In the story Pavel told, he was fourteen. Art filled the apartment. Canvases leaned against the couch, were stacked against one another by the walls. Pavel's paintings had just begun to resemble his father's. His father squeezed out a tube of blue paint. "Hear that?" he kept asking, glancing at the door. His mother winced from the arm of the couch. It wasn't until later that Pavel would realize his parents had been expecting the Secret Police.

Pavel had been painting a gray man for a half hour when the doorbell rang unmistakably. His father sent him into the bathroom to wash and smeared his own hands with paint. Pavel hurried. When he got out of the bathroom, his mother took his arm. Two men hovered in their living room like birds, sharp-beaked and feathered in plaid.

"Please sit down," the first bird said, as if it were his house. He asked what Pavel's father was painting.

"Just a woman in the fog," his father said. Pavel hid his disappointment. The figure was a man.

The first bird asked if Pavel's father was changing his style.

"I'm going to look around," the second bird said. He walked into the other rooms.

"There's a lot of variety in these paintings," the first bird said. He searched the stacks. Pavel could smell how clean the man was, as if he'd just taken a shower, through the muddy smell of his jacket. The jacket didn't seem right, as if it belonged to someone else.

As his partner emerged from the bedroom, the first bird said, "I would hate to have to take them away."

"What do you know about the *Vybor na obranu nespravedlivě stíhaných*?" the second bird asked Pavel's father.

His father was still holding the brush and palette. He put these down and joined Pavel and his mother. "I know that if you put me in jail," he said, "the *Vybor na obranu nespravedlivě stíhaných* will know about it."

"But why would they put you in jail, Táta?" Pavel asked. His mother's grip loosened as if he had fallen away from her.

His father said they would put him in jail because they felt threatened by him. "Always remember that," he said. "*I* am dangerous to *them*."

The second bird laughed. Pavel's mother said, "Not my husband," as if agreeing with the bird.

The first bird stepped around Pavel's painting and wiped his finger across it: a gray streak. He tapped a fingerprint in the middle of the fog, and said, "Tell me which paintings are yours."

"They're all mine," Pavel's father said, resting his hand on Pavel's shoulder.

Pavel felt his father's grip tighten, saw his father's eyebrows scrunch together, but still he felt ashamed. His father had claimed his bad art. He felt worse than he could reason or hope away. His arm hurt from people holding him, but he found it impossible to complain. It was as if his father stood alone with the bird-men now, as if his mother and he didn't exist, his arm didn't exist.

"You're not building a little army inside your home?" the first bird asked.

"The boy can't paint," his father said. "He never learned. He's horrible."

Something burned behind Pavel's eyes. He looked away from the bird-men. Outside, the fog was the same as in his painting. Then he could smell tears running down his face, greasy and sour, though he was far too old to cry. Even later, when he understood his father had meant to protect him, the memory of those words could make him well up.

The two bird-men were quiet now, and Pavel's parents were quiet, his sniffling the only sound. Finally the first bird shrugged and pushed Pavel's father toward the door. "I guess he means it," he said. The second bird flipped open a knife, slashed a few canvases from their frames, and stuffed them under his arm.

V

In the hospital in Boston, Tee would remember Pavel's story. Somehow, he hadn't seen the rage in it. He had imagined Pavel as a little boy who felt betrayed. He'd forgotten the Pavel telling the story, the man who understood his father and held on to the memory because that was the day his father was taken from him, unavenged.

At the end of February, Tee picked up the evening shifts at an English bookstore, the Globe, which stayed open late to serve coffee and beer in the adjoining café. He liked how the staff would read aloud, like songbirds calling to one another in sonorous paragraphs. In the interview, he sat in a tiny office overflowing with stock. Boxes of books covered the desk, only a thin gap in the middle through which two people could see each other. A short-haired girl with an endearing lisp sat across from Tee and asked his favorite book. When he mentioned *Clea*, she smiled and pushed a box aside. She unclasped a green barrette and pinned her dark hair higher on her head. He told her how his mother had worked part-time at a library, the musty scent of the stacks. He rested his hand on a poetry book with a lifeguard on the cover. He admired how the woman's, Ynez's, voice seemed to crest into questions like a wave. For some reason he told her about the set of encyclopedias his uncle had given him on his tenth birthday. He was supposed to write down what he learned each day. His uncle had taped one of Tee's notes inside the cockpit of a favorite plane. *Airplanes fly by obstruction. The air that flows over the round top of the wing has to flow even faster than the particles abandoned beneath.* His uncle had underlined *obstruction.* Tee wondered whether the celebrities his uncle had piloted around had ever seen what he had written.

Ynez had moved to Prague from New York, in July. They got to talking about America. She told him one of her friends had worked in the World Trade Center; her friend's dog had fallen ill the morning of the attack, and she had taken the dog to the vet instead of going to work.

Tee tapped his fingers on the desk. The chair bit into his back. Then he found himself saying that his uncle had flown a plane into the ground while his family was distracted by the attacks, that his father and his aunt had caused the suicide. As Ynez put a book in his hands, he saw that he was trembling. For a moment her eyes seemed as blue as Katka's. She fluttered her five fingers through the air. "What is this?" she asked. He shook his head. She said, "A flock of these," and repeated the pattern with only her pinky. "Why do seagulls fly over the ocean and not the bay?" she asked. "Because then they would be bagels." He wanted to pull her toward him and hold those jokes in his arms. He didn't know why she offered him the job.

He intended, at first, to read for his final semester: biographies of Romantic poets for his undergraduate thesis. Instead he bought fabulist novels and books of myths and fables. More real than life. The passages the staff read aloud shared a disconnectedness, a lonesomeness, characters lost in changing worlds. Maybe because they, the staff, faced such misunderstandings in Prague. Once, on the Bridge of Legions, a man in a patched coat had taken an apple from Tee's hand before Tee could eat it, pulled a switchblade from the coat, and sliced the fruit open to a star pattern, nodding gravely. "Good luck," the man said,

"Asian." Tee didn't know if the man was wishing him luck or calling his race lucky. Unlike the others, though, Tee trusted Prague's strangeness. Ynez was the only one at the Globe like him. She had planned to travel through Europe, but had changed her plans after a single walk through Old Town, a giant metronome ticking on the hill above. She told Tee that the star was lucky. Soon he was coming in an hour early so their schedules overlapped.

Once the paintings of Tee were finished, Pavel's friend Rockefeller helped look for an art dealer who could arrange an exhibit in New York. The revenue would go to a new café the friends had decided to open in the fall. Tee didn't know what to say about the paintings of him traveling the opposite route he had come. His desire to keep being painted, like his job, was mostly a desire not to disappear. He continued to visit the house in Malešice. Sometimes Pavel squinted at Tee in the doorway, as if trying to recall what he had seen on New Year's. But he didn't offer another thank-you painting or mention that Tee could or should stop coming. Each morning on the tram, Tee would jot down things to say, wanting to contribute without art. They would sit around the kitchen table as if in a café. Occasionally Pavel would drift into the bedroom to paint, and Tee, alone with Katka, would try to deny the floating sensation: as if they were two boats tied to the same dock.

The afternoon that Pavel announced Rockefeller had found an American dealer, Katka clunked her empty teacup on its saucer and said she missed the old distribution, hanging the paintings in public, inspiring people to action. She had to disagree, once again, that a gallery in New York was a better venue than Prague. The cup rattled the saucer—somehow she was still holding it delicately. Then she muttered something indelicate in Czech. Pavel stormed into the bedroom. It was the first time Tee had seen them fight.

Dishes littered the table: the aftermath of fresh bread, gulaš soup, tea, merciless appetites. On the dishes were paintings Pavel's father had done: portraits of the family in the 1970s, his only personal pieces.

"Cimrman invented the airplane cabin but had to wait for someone to invent an airplane," Katka said to Tee. She tore off a piece of bread but didn't eat it. "Pavel has forgotten the Czech sensibility. Yours are his first political paintings since Communism, and the best."

"They aren't mine." Tee imagined Andy Warhol at the table.

Katka drifted to the window. The fringe of her skirt brushed his side. "The model is the painting's ex-lover," she said. "The artist is its current one." Some admission gathered behind her eyes, but quickly disappeared.

As she touched the glass, Tee remembered: wrong women. But he reached toward her waist.

"What are you doing?" she said sharply.

They heard something crash in the other room. His uncle's plane, twisted, in flames.

After a moment Katka said, "I love him," as if to answer a question Tee hadn't asked.

Later that evening, in the Globe, Tee ran his finger along a row of book spines as Ynez organized the shelf beside his counter. He took down a book and read. *The presence of want awakens in him nostalgia for wholeness.* He knew desire was just around the corner. What kept it hidden—setting? time? Ynez shifted her hips toward him. He couldn't talk in the Globe about what it felt like to be painted, to be *seen*. He never mentioned Pavel and Katka to Ynez. Around her, his container got all mixed up. He told her about his father's "business trips"; his aunt, at the funeral, glancing over her bony shoulder as if waiting to be accused. He asked Ynez what it might mean if someone said he was holding a door open for himself, and then closed it. She was quiet for a while. Finally she said, "Sometimes our passion is so strong that it makes a fool of us." Her Castilian lisp (she had grown up in Spain before studying sociology at Cornell) made him lean in to catch every word. She evened the books on the shelf until she was inches from his face. Why did he want to stay here, he asked himself again, in Prague? Heat breathed from her skin. She was probably an expert on passion, her parted lips and long lashes. He imagined pulling her into the stacks, a corner of books no one ever looked for. "Your Anne Carson has written plenty about that." Slowly she pivoted and rested her slim white arms on the desk. "Though, I don't know, I'm not saying we don't make the choice of who to love for ourselves."

"We don't make the choice for ourselves," Tee repeated. He clasped his hands behind his back. "In Boston I dated older women who must have reminded me of my aunt."

"I know what you're thinking," Ynez said after a moment. "You don't have to prove yourself."

He wasn't trying to prove himself, though. He suppressed a strong urge to share a story about his childhood: a night he had spent alone in the woods, because he was six and had thought he could find his birth mother there. "You know what I want more than anything else?" he said. "I want to be old, and to rock on the porch with my wife. To look back and have everything figured out."

"You want to skip your youth?" she lisped.

He took a pen from his shirt pocket and drew on a bookmark. "At the time you make a decision, you have no idea how it will turn out. Life would be so much easier if you knew what you could do with it."

Ynez reached for the pen and tucked it above her ear. On the bookmark, a baby lay at a man's feet. She frowned. "You mean like holding the door for yourself?"

He swept the bookmark away from her. He felt stung, like he had slapped a little kid and she had caught him, like she had seen him go too far.

He made an effort, and rested his fingertips on her wrist. He could feel her pulse quicken. "I may have to go back for a few days. My mom is set on divorce. She keeps e-mailing me that she means it."

"Don't worry," Ynez said. "Your job will still be here when you get back."

VI

Once Ynez had left, Tee touched the books she had touched, his fingers still with the warmth of her wrist. In the story he'd wanted to tell her, he had run away from home with a photo of his birth mother.

His parents lived in a renovated farmhouse outside of Boston, the yard bordering a forest where lost dogs were often found. When he was a boy, those woods had seemed to him a fairy world where anything was possible. The winter he turned six, he had a sharp feeling, like an earache, and while his parents fought over his father's latest indiscretion, he pocketed the sole photograph of his birth mother and snuck into the snow-glistened trees.

The black-and-white Polaroid was the one thing Tee had from Korea, proof he was hers. He'd already memorized her face against his own (her softer angles, her darker skin). He'd memorized the smell, plastic with the slightest trace of coffee—maybe his father had spilled on it. On the back of the photo, his father had written the three syllables she'd said before she died, *Kang Seul Peum*. In the woods Tee chanted these syllables like a spell. He made a circle of snowballs around him. He wondered if, as his father had guessed, she had tried to name him. For a while, under the snow-bent trees, Tee enjoyed the anticipation. He imagined his mother appearing in a blue flame, like in a cartoon he had seen. But once the sun set, the universe shifted. His fingers froze, and the snow blew and melted against his cheeks like tears. He recalled the Medusa from his father's book of myths, able to turn a boy to stone. All night he waited for some monster to find him, and in the morning, as he made his way to a neighbor's house in the half-light, cold and sick and wet, the photo had lost its protection.

When he got home, his mother called his father in from the woods. Tee heard a flashlight flick off in the foyer. They rubbed his body until he stopped shivering, but they couldn't halt the march of illness. Pneumonia weakened him, flooding his lungs until it got hard to breathe, and when red dots burst on his chest, they discovered he'd caught chicken pox as well, from school. In two weeks he lost ten of his fifty pounds. He dreamed of his birth mother stretchered into the hospital, dying, like on TV. She reached for a tall American with a broken leg. Had they made a pact? Her hand covered his, and it was agreed. The half-pale boy emerging in a mix of afterbirth and death would go to America.

For a while, after the flood, Prague would seem to gather back up inside Tee, piece by piece. The paintings. Katka's legends. Ynez's warmth. Ghosts. The problem was, there had always been something itching inside him, fluttering like a bird in his throat, waiting to fly out. He didn't know when the itching had started. He had felt it in those woods when he was six.

In the Globe, as Tee opened a book about Prague's river sprites, he sensed someone behind him. He was almost afraid to turn around. He remembered the spell of the syllables, how simple his adoption had seemed to him as a boy. His father had fallen in love with him—in the hospital in Korea, after watching his birth mother die—and had taken responsibility for Tee's life. Even that time Tee got sick, when a priest arrived to give the last rites, his father had walked in, put one hand on the priest's shoulder and the other on his son's cheek, and stopped death.

A statuesque Czech stooped under the archway separating the steps down to the bookstore from the open space of the café. It was Rockefeller.

Back when Tee had started modeling, Rockefeller had helped him rent an apartment across the hall in the same building in Karlín, an up-and-coming district east of the Jewish Quarter. As neighbors, they had formed a hesitant friendship. Tee remembered drinking with Rockefeller after the protest against the former prime minister's acquittal, the one that Pavel and Katka had also gone to. They had to meet aboveground, not in one of the wine cellars Tee was drawn to. Rockefeller stood a thick six foot six, with cabbage-sized shoulders and a shock of brown hair like a toupee, which often displaced light fixtures. By the third Budvar, Rockefeller was bragging about how he had used his university's press to print samizdats full of Pavel's paintings—before anyone knew Pavel other than by his father. "You know how he got name Picasso?" Rockefeller asked Tee. The waitress passed by, and Rockefeller lowered his voice, as if they were in danger, and said he had used his parents' Party connections. He had tricked them and leaked a samizdat to the foreign press.

Tee didn't know what to make of this brag. Rockefeller was clearly tricking himself. His parents had been high-level Communists who fled the country after the Revolution. They must have known that Communism would end. They had given Rockefeller his name by special permission.

Rockefeller ordered another round. Tee doodled the Czech flag on a napkin, then slipped the napkin into his wallet, as if it would work away there, writing over his Americanness.

In the Globe, Rockefeller's head hung forward and he held the lapel of his sports jacket closed. He led Tee away from the stacks to a table by the main entrance—the Globe was in a century-old building with bronze banisters and a vaulted ceiling in the front section. Rockefeller ordered them beers and pulled from his bag a hand-drawn blueprint of his and Pavel's future café. "Advising me," he said, that same Shakespearean heft to his accent, as if aping the artist. "I want that everyone will come. Americans will come, then everyone."

His eyes never wavered from Tee's, two round bulges above his caved cheeks and square chin: a face that seemed composed more of a theme than of genetic traits. Sometimes Tee liked feeling swept along in the current of Rockefeller's self-assurance. Yet the relentless eye contact, those cabbage shoulders, the way Rockefeller rattled the blueprint in Tee's face and asked for money, unsettled him. Tee regretted mentioning his inheritance as proof he could pay his rent.

"I told you I'm not an investor," he said. "My uncle died just six months ago."

"You'll changing mind. Here, look at this. I'm putting space for talking here. Real talking needs this shape of room. And Pavel's paintings. Here, on wall, Picasso."

There was beer on Rockefeller's breath, and he could go on about Pavel Picasso for hours if drunk. Tee had to change the subject. But he said, "Paintings of Katka? I've seen them in the museums. Are they all of her?"

Rockefeller touched thumb to forefinger. "I'm putting them together."

"A perfect couple?" Tee asked.

Tee couldn't picture this giant match-making. Rockefeller smoothed his lapel and asked how anyone could be perfect. Then, as if he had just thought of it, he said, "Why Prague? Why not you going to Korea?"

Tee had heard this question from the bookstore staff, from Pavel. He sketched spire after spire on his coaster, under an empty sky. In Korea there was nothing for him that wasn't already buried deep underground. "Stop drawing," Rockefeller said, covering the pen with his hand.

"Pavel and Katka aren't perfect?" Tee asked again.

"*Proč?*" Rockefeller said. "Why, you wanting her?"

Tee was relieved he'd already reddened from the alcohol. His Asian blush.

Rockefeller pulled his hand away and studied the blueprint, laughing. But after a sip of beer, he fell silent. Tee's breaths quickened. For some reason he couldn't look up. He scooped the drawing into his lap. The café seemed to grow louder, busier. Then a woman walked in—the daughter of Pavel's art dealer, a New Yorker full of the indifference of skyscrapers—and glanced around until she found them. She adjusted her skirt and waved. Rockefeller crumpled the blueprint in one bearish paw.

"What's Vanessa doing here?" Tee asked.

The paper lay crippled on the table as Vanessa strode toward them. "I need that money," Rockefeller whispered, "please."

That same evening, Tee sat on the edge of his bed, in the dark, as Rockefeller knocked at his door. Tee recalled how Rockefeller's fingers, on the café table, curled into fat fists. On the bed lay the blueprint, the creases smoothed flat. Tee had taken it. He shivered, aware of how stupid it was to be hiding, and from what? He would run into Rockefeller the next day, or the next.

When the knocking stopped, Tee waited for fifteen minutes, and then he called Ynez and got out of the building. Ynez said she had wanted him to call for a while, but wasn't he going to America soon? They talked and talked, until it was clear he was not returning to his apartment.

VII

On the last day of March, Tee would again meet the artist and the artist's wife in Old Town Square. He was walking back to Karlín, not watching where he was going, when a colorful wing dropped on his shoulder. The Thai Massage parrot grinned and repeated that Tee was Thai. It was so sudden that Tee slipped and caught his hand on the cobblestone. His container filled. He wished to accept this strangeness, but for some reason he could not. At that moment, someone shouted in Czech and the parrot flapped off, fearing the tall woman—it was Katka. Like on New Year's, she had appeared when Tee needed someone. She helped him up, and his pulse sprang to her touch. Pavel walked out of a nearby shop. She squeezed Tee's hand. They were running errands, shopping for Pavel's café. He and Rockefeller were going to choose a location the next morning. Tee said casually that he could keep Katka company while Pavel was out. Pavel stomped his cigarette, closed his hands in his armpits, and said they could have a "see you alligator" party.

That night, Katka appeared in Tee's dreams again and again, until he could see her flaws. The hint of cruelty in her stare. One side of her body slightly longer than the other. In one dream she was Korean.

She led him up to a rooftop. From the roof Tee could see Boston, his ex-girlfriend mouthing, "Wrong woman." His nose itched, and he scratched until it fell off in his palm. Upon descending the staircase, he and Katka were inside his apartment in Karlín. He switched on the lights; she switched them off. When he tried to speak, the words exited his lips, like tiny scraps of paper, and entered hers. He woke aching with desire.

In the morning, he rode the tram to Malešice. The entire winter, his painted selves had hopped out of their canvases and into his sleep as if to offer other lives, or as ghosts of lives he'd already lived somewhere else. He wondered which of those canvases Katka would say was most like him. He trusted her instinctively.

In the first, he shone with faith beside the Orloj as he left his feet.

In the second, a black bird clawed his shoulder, its feathers shiny and metallic. He lit its tail like a rocket, waiting for it to explode.

In the third, he stood at a mirror. The canvas was long and wide. In the mirror was Old Town, his reflection half-naked in the night streets, and in the corner, a door.

In the fourth, Pavel had exaggerated Tee. As tall and skinny as a skyscraper, as brown as a wet sand castle. But his eyes were not his. They were blue.

From the tram stop, Tee walked down to Pavel and Katka's yard, past the gnarled maple tree she loved, and knocked at the kitchen door. She opened it, aproned. The scent of gulaš and cabbage trailed her like a loyal pet. Her stare flashed past him at first, then focused on his face. She pursed her lips in an incomprehensible whistle. On an impulse, he shook her hand, and she smiled at his awkwardness. She had bladelike cheekbones, sharp enough to halt a trespasser in his tracks.

They sat at the kitchen table, out of habit, and ate slowly. He asked about the paintings, and she said the first was the best. After he'd praised her cooking a third time, she said, "I want to know something about you that no one else knows."

He wasn't sure what to tell her, and then he was talking about his father's affair. "You want to know why I left Boston? My uncle committed suicide. Afterward I searched my dad's office. I needed some sign of who he really was. He was always filming things. I pulled these boxes down from the top of his closet, and inside were old textbooks, geology books he probably knew by heart. It was a strange place for them. I got this hunch, and when I emptied the last box, in the very bottom was a reel of film older than I am." He waited for her to comment on the suicide or his age, but she ignored both.

He told himself to shut up. Was he trying to relate to her or to warn her? He knew, suddenly, how he gazed at her, why he had dreamed of her. Yet he had chosen Ynez.

"You can tell me what was on it," she said, sliding her hand over the table onto his with scary timing.

"Forget it." He dipped a dumpling into the sauce and ate it. "It's not something about me, it's about my dad."

He remembered hooking up the old projector as his father had taught him. He had known from the tightness in his chest, even before the film flickered on, to lock the door.

"I will not force you to talk," Katka said. Her hand was cold.

"On the film was my dad telling my aunt that my mom couldn't get pregnant."

After a moment Katka said, "And?"

Tee coughed with surprise. He tried to move for his beer, but Katka held him still. "You want to know?" he said. His father's dream had always been to make films, documentaries where the camera was the eye of the beholder. He was obsessed with this idea, a way of seeing twice. The film Tee had found held two perspectives: his father's and his aunt's. The screen shook as his aunt recorded his father.

I married Zoe because she understood me. But that wasn't enough.

Tee tried to reach for his beer again. Katka didn't let go. She wanted to stand beside him in his memories. She wanted his past. When his aunt had come on screen, her sunken cheeks, she had said, *It's not your fault.* Then her arm had stretched out, and the screen went black.

Katka held Tee's hand until he didn't think of pulling away anymore. He kept silent. He had come to Prague to resist. "The thing," he said finally, "no one else knows about me is that I like you."

He refused to blush or look away.

Her grip tightened, and then it eased and she began to sweat. He had rattled her for a second. "So young," she said softly. "Come on. I want to show you something." And like in his dream, she led him into the bedroom.

She'd cleaned the paint-specked newspaper off the floor. The hardwood gleamed. When she opened the closet, he saw immediately. Inside were dozens of paintings, each of a part or the whole of her body. She flicked on the light and pushed him in, though there was barely room to stand. She surrounded him, the same ivory of her skin, the same sharp cheeks and penetrating blue irises. He was in a room of mirrors reflecting only her.

"Pavel painted these," he said.

She nodded.

"Why are they hidden away in here?" To his left, her pink nipples winked at him.

"He does not think they are good enough." She came up behind him and lifted his elbow. His fingers brushed one of the canvases. Her face and neck and shoulders. He felt the rough brushstrokes that made the smooth look of her skin. Her hand moved up his forearm, nudging him closer. "He has always painted me. From the very beginning. The paintings of me in museums are distortions. These are the truer ones, which he refuses to show."

Tee saw how important Pavel's art was to her. Pictures of her had helped make a revolution. That was love. She would never let that go. She was sharing a secret, but a secret between her and Pavel. On the back of the closet door hung a long sketch of her body, nude.

"You do not know what he was like then," she said. "He was brilliant. People responded to him, and he took the attention and turned it into something useful. Art was useful then. His more than any other." She touched a spot on the painting, too, tenderly, like she'd never touched it before. An inch above where Tee's finger had been. He was reminded that she was a little taller than he. Then she swept her arm out as if to include all the paintings in what she had said.

"Rockefeller told me," Tee said. "Pavel is someone to entrust a nation to."

"He was."

As Katka lowered her arm, Tee registered the tense. *Is. Was.* "So sweet and so young," she muttered. Then she was kissing him, her tongue parting his lips, her hands already clutching his back. He shut his eyes and leaned into her. He pushed her up against the images of herself, or she drew him down on top of them. She was a rough kisser, biting his lips. She said something he didn't catch. She tasted like almonds, though they hadn't eaten almonds. It was strange, how he could feel his veins. He had never felt his veins before. She made him more aware of himself. She slipped one hand under his belt. She licked his throat and wrapped her fingers around his limp penis. Then across the frame of the door darted someone's shadow. Katka stroked him, trying to make him hard, but the shadow glowed in the hall.

"Stop," Tee managed. "Your husband."

She bit his earlobe. "Do not be stupid."

He pushed out of her closet, past the images of her body and into the bedroom. In the hall he dusted off his clothes as if his desire had stuck to him.

No one was there.

"What is wrong with you?" she said, behind him.

He remembered Pavel's father imagining the Secret Police at the door. She spun him around, and he thought now she would continue kissing him and he would never be able to stop. But she only glared and told him to get his coat.

VIII

Tee took a cab from the airport. The Massachusetts Turnpike gave way to tree-lined streets and then the big brown farmhouse where he had grown up. Their driveway was full of cars he'd never seen before, the lawn full of people. A yard sale. When he got out of the cab, he found boxes full of his father's things. This was the reason his mother couldn't pick him up.

He'd surprised her, coming home. He hadn't wanted to call from Prague, to hear her voice echo off the cobblestone. Now the familiar smells of a Boston spring—the leaves that had fallen in autumn at last thawing and decomposing, the firm soil still cold with the memory of snow, and, of course, the flowers—surrounded him.

Tee pecked his mother's cheek. The couple browsing his father's DVDs eyed them. An Asian kid kissing an older white woman. Wrong women. "When is Dad getting home?" he asked. "Does he know about this?"

His father was in Oregon, surveying land for a thermal spa, supposedly his last job for a while. His mother was sorry the sale had to be today. It was the start of April, spring-cleaning, and she had been planning this for weeks. Tee stacked up old film reels and carried them past her pitying glare into the house.

His father's office was completely bare. A pale square on the wall marked where the projection screen had hung, always down, in use. Tee had watched his father's first film, *POV*, on that screen. His father's idée fixe: dozens of scenes from different viewpoints—their neighbors', Tee's uncle's, his mother's, his aunt's. In high school Tee had spent hours secretly poring through old home videos, going back in time from middle school debates to their rare family vacations, to his birthday parties at mini-golf courses, to his parents moving into the farmhouse for the first time, their life together still full of hope. In one of the early videos, his mother turns to the camera: "I'm tired of this." Whirling and sighing. "Today I'll play the role of the wife who finally says what she thinks. I'm skipping ahead. Damn your brother for buying you that camcorder. I want to be more than an imaginary woman." The focus is up close. When she moves, his father has to follow quickly, has to anticipate where she's going—yet he never seems in danger of losing her.

"He moved into a hotel about a month ago," his mother said now, from the doorway, brushing her forehead as if to sweep away the freckles. "He stays there when he's in town."

Tee dropped the reels on the windowsill and pulled the shade so the light wouldn't fade them. When he turned back, his mother was in tears. "Give me one good reason not to leave him," she said.

He tried to think of something to negate the affair. He couldn't. He kept picturing his father chewing the insides of his cheeks at his uncle's funeral. "Remember you said Dad tried to film my adoption day, the whole family together, but Uncle Hi never came?" he said. "How it turned out Auntie had threatened to jump off the roof that afternoon? Remember Dad called you after I hit my chin with that toy car, and you argued so long I didn't get stitches fast enough?" He lifted one hand to his chin as his father would, and rested the other in the middle of the faded square. "We're family. No matter how much we hurt each other. You can't do this."

"These last six months," his mother started. Her freckles darkened. "I remember everything. Everything."

That night, after Tee had rescued what he could from the yard, he lay in his childhood bed. He felt the sink spot in his mattress, under his waist. He recalled his father's voice cracking on the phone in September. Almost seven months had passed, but Tee could still see everything clearly. He was molding Reynolds Wrap to the TV antenna in his studio apartment in Brighton. The breeze took hold of the foil like windmill blades; he pricked his finger trying to set it. On the phone his father said a farmer had found the wreckage of his uncle's plane in a wheat field in upper New York. A week after the terror attacks. Shock buzzed on the line, as if Tee could uncap the receiver and something would fly out and sting him. He asked whether the crash had anything to do with 9/11. His father didn't answer. Tee would have to find out from his mother that it was suicide.

As he shifted his weight on his bed, Tee remembered how, as a boy, he had wanted his uncle's rough pilot hands; he'd once burned himself trying to make calluses. He remembered how his uncle had shaved his lumberjack beard, and they had scattered the hair over Boston. His uncle could make anything a mystery: blisters, beards, surrender.

Finally Tee stumbled downstairs and turned on his mother's computer in the den, the Internet so easily at his fingertips. He wouldn't contact his friends. They would only ask why he hadn't earlier, or why he was home at all. He sat in his boxers and Googled his uncle's name, finding nothing new. He read the news from Afghanistan. In Prague it was nearly morning; soon the city would turn grain-gold, rippling with sunlight. He found an article in the *Boston Globe* about a suicide gene.

How long had his uncle battled that gene within himself, or had the enemy for him always been life? The past more alive than the present. Like a ghost. Or like how Tee always reverted, in his parents' house, to a little boy. When he felt exhausted of the Internet, Tee held up one of his father's film reels to a flashlight, frame by frame. His uncle stood by the plane he'd started his business with, grinning as he always did in the air. It had been a huge bank loan that could have crushed him. He cut a disembodied ribbon. The camera moved over the shining metal, across his uncle's arm to that familiar bearded face. Then, in a couple of frames, something strange happened. For what was merely an instant in film time, his uncle's expression shifted and he looked—those fifteen years ago—like a man who was always going to kill himself. A few frames later, he seemed again brimming with life. Tee felt desperate to return to Prague.

When his father came back, two days later, Tee drove his mother's SUV to the hotel. His father stepped into the hall, closing the door behind him. "You won't let me in?" Tee asked. They talked for a minute about the thermal spa in Oregon, until Tee said, "What are you hiding?"

Inside, penciled movie frames covered the walls, sweeping drawings of towers and eyes and a plane broken in a field. The drawings curled up the walls, almost to the ceiling. Tee wondered how his father had reached up there. He stared for a long time. Was this how a person lost his mind? Only his family could have recognized what his father had drawn. The old fixations. After the crash, when his uncle's death received minimal coverage, his father had called the local news stations and begged them to see his point of view—their personal tragedy lost in the scope of the towers. As Tee studied the drawings, he remembered being painted in Prague, his doodling on napkins and coasters. What was his connection to these walls? To his father? They shared no genetics, yet he felt as if these frames could be running in his own mind. He couldn't let them.

His father dropped his chin and whispered an apology, as if what he should be sorry for was re-creating what had happened, not what had happened itself. Tee was the adult now. Their roles had switched. He was bringing home the boy who had run away. Except his father had been kicked out.

"You know your mom checked your auntie into an institution?"

Tee opened the closet, expecting to find more sketches. "Was it easy?" he asked. "To love someone else? Your brother's wife?" Only clothing, hung neatly for a long stay.

His father twitched his long nose, raised an eyebrow.

At the wake, Tee's aunt had run to the urn screaming that she should be inside, it was all her fault. No one had restrained her. Then everyone had.

"Were you happier with her?" Tee asked, pulling down a suit.

"I'm still your dad," his father said.

"Was she happier with you?"

Finally his father sat on the bed, shivering in the air-conditioning, in April. Tee tried to imagine the guilt of causing a brother's death. But his father, as always, was in denial.

"The hangers aren't mine," his father said.

Tee threw everything on the floor, a heap of creases. His container emptied. "Since when have you worried about what's yours or not?" he shouted. He thought for a second of the closet full of paintings of Katka, the feel of the thick brushstrokes under his fingers, the shadow in the hall.

As they packed and erased his father's drawings, Tee held his tongue. His father was confused. It was like the week his father had lain in bed, speaking gibberish, after having his wisdom teeth removed, like a teenager. Dry sockets and codeine. Tee was nine. His mother mixed milk shakes. His aunt came over. One morning his father stared into the room and said hello in Korean, *Annyeong haseyo*, and they all turned to see who it was, he seemed so sure. Another time, he looked at Tee's aunt and said, "Zoe." His aunt reddened. Tee's mother smiled and asked what she could do. It had always been like that with his father: you never knew where you stood.

On the drive back to the house, the suitcases banging in the trunk, a plane flew low overhead. His father said his uncle's hangar had been sold.

Tee had stacked the boxes he'd saved from the yard sale in his father's office; he moved his father in among his old things. His mother stared from the hall and clicked her teeth together. His father's cheeks hung like a bulldog's as she listed what she deserved in the divorce. She rapped her nails against the wood with each item. Car. House. Peace of mind.

Each time Tee entered the office, his father had sketched another scene across the walls. "Memory lives longer than anything else," his father said. He turned and seemed to breathe in the pencil, then rested his forehead where the projection screen had hung, in the same spot Tee had put his hand. "You can't change it."

"But you can change your life," Tee said.

"I've been paying for you to stay in Prague," his father said, rubbing his neck.

"But now you don't have to. Now Uncle Hi will."

Around two o'clock in the morning, Tee went downstairs for a glass of milk and paused on the bottom step. Something glinted under the porch light. The door was open. He heard a muted swear. The glint was the tripod to his father's camcorder. For a moment it stuck on the threshold; then, with a grunt, it was gone. Tee didn't move. If he did, seeing his father run away would become real. He imagined his father waving at the house one last time before getting into the car. In front of Tee, on the hardwood floor, a white square of paper fluttered. The shutting door had kicked up a tiny wind. The note said his father was taking his share of the inheritance to Hollywood.

When Tee called the next day, his father said Tee just couldn't understand. That, perhaps, was true.

On his last day in Boston, Tee e-mailed his adviser that he was abandoning his thesis. A hundred pages on the poetry of an Age? He was turning to older stories, stories people had told for centuries. Compared to the culture of revelation (in poetry, in the news, in life), myth was constant. As an afterthought, Tee cited his uncle's death. He needed more time to move on. His adviser couldn't question that.

Later Tee thought maybe a disappearing act was the one trick their family had mastered.

At the airport, his mother laid her palm on his chest and said, "Your father." She chewed her lip. Tee remembered tugging a yellow sundress, trying to pull her into the waves on the Cape. She'd dipped her whole long body under—he searched for her yellow blur. When she popped up, far from shore, he waded out, scared she would leave him. But later, on the drive home, he had wished to swim like her. Able to stroke out and reach the distant side.

That same day, he remembered now, they had stopped in Hyannis for their favorite ice cream, his father's and his. His mother had gone ahead. A group of tourists passed by, laughing about something, and his father pulled Tee into an alley. Tee couldn't see anything out of the ordinary about them. What frightened him was that his father cupped his face and whispered, "I will never let anyone take you," as if one of them was going to try. When his mother found them, she said, "I guess you told him." But afterward, nothing changed.

Now his mother's palm fell away from Tee's chest. The brown of her freckles deepened. "Don't be like him," she said. "Don't disappear. And don't forget who you are."

On the plane, he cupped his cheek and imagined his father, then rested his hands on his chest where his mother's had been. His much darker hands, the hands of a foreign diplomat, perhaps, of a Korean farm girl. Tee had the brief thought that he should go farther east and never return.

CHAPTER 2
GHOSTS

I

In September 2002, after his father flew him back from Prague for good, Tee would stand at the window in Massachusetts General Hospital and stare out at the river for hours. At night he dreamed of floodwater. He smelled something rotting in the distance. For an instant he caught a woman's silhouette behind the frosted glass that separated him from the hall. Then, on the floor, a pair of boots glowed. When he picked up the boots, water poured out of them. The door was locked. He couldn't reach the woman, though she couldn't have gone far. The room felt smaller, or was closing in; he hadn't noticed how small it was before. He would wake screaming his own name, as if he stood outside with the woman and couldn't save himself, as if the water was inside him. Even after he woke, a ghostly calf curved around his door again and again.

In August, in Prague, the flood would seem a surprise, though storms came and went for weeks beforehand. Police and firefighters raised steel barriers along the embankments in Old Town but left the Karlín district unprotected. On the news a former construction worker warned that buildings in Karlín could collapse, built too quickly—with unfired bricks. An analyst predicted deaths and lawsuits. The city surrendered its boundaries. Citizens defended museums and places of worship with sandbags. In the rain an evacuation was ordered, but people thronged to bridges and riverbanks to watch. Sections of sidewalk buckled like tiny tectonic plates. Trees tipped over in the oversaturated soil and had to be tethered like barges. Metro lines were shut down too late to protect them. The river washed parts of other cities into Prague. The river pulled down levees, then buildings. The river washed parts of Prague into other parts of Prague, then into the rest of Europe.

From where Tee watched in his second-floor apartment, the flood made a high brown sea just below his window. He smelled the sewage in the water. He wondered how he had let himself miss the signs. How strange the way we wade into disaster, step after step, not realizing how far we've gone until we're drowning.

Just before the flood, Katka had asked about Korea as the raindrops formed fat planets against the windowpane. Her finger followed the streaks across the glass.

"A Korean friend told me once about his visits as a kid," Tee said. "Everyone looked like him, but he still didn't belong."

Katka touched her temple where her skin met her hair. "No one your age," she said, "feels like he belongs."

This was the same woman who had cursed at the Thai massage parrot. How did she really see him: his quick black eyes, the scar on his chin that toughened his boyishness, his flat cheeks and curved nose, the cream in his brown skin that seemed to make white people touch him without realizing. He was a believer, as Pavel had painted. In college he had listed ambitions: get a girlfriend, be a writer, drink more water, fall in love. He had believed in the kind of weight that could drag whatever fluttered in his throat down to more comfortable depths—a someplace or a someone.

Katka smoothed her hair, and he said, "You don't know what it's like to be adopted. People see you as who you were at birth. But you're not that person."

At that point, the flood was still weeks off. He opened the window and caught rain in the cup of his palm. Katka pulled his hand in, and for a moment, he thought for some reason that she would lower her lips to the water and drink. She splashed his face. He pulled back in anger, but her grin conquered him.

When Tee got back to Prague, in April, he holed up in his apartment for several days before he was scheduled to work again. He talked to Ynez on the phone, and asked for some time alone. He had bought a Czech art book before he left, and he dog-eared the pages on Pavel's paintings. Distorted versions of Katka. He would go out, he decided, when he could look at those paintings and not think about his father and his aunt. Finally he called to ask Pavel and Katka to drinks. Tee wondered what Katka had told her husband about that morning in the closet. Hopefully nothing. Katka said Pavel would go for drinks, but she would not. She added nothing else. "I've realized something," Tee said. She hung up.

That night, Pavel and Rockefeller met Tee and Ynez at a bar in Vyšehrad with a flying horse on the sign. Tee told them about the impending divorce. Rockefeller told awkward sympathy jokes and Pavel was stony. "Now who will raising you?" Pavel asked, as if Tee was still a little boy. Though she didn't have to, Ynez said Tee would raise himself. They ordered round after round. Ynez told a joke about a man who sprays his lawn for tigers. *But there aren't any tigers around*, says his wife, and the man says, *See? It's working*. After their sixth round, Rockefeller asked about the inheritance. His intimidating bulk, which had once saved Pavel at a political rally, pinballed around the bar. At one point he gripped the edge of a counter built into the wall, and the wood creaked in his hand. Tee stepped in front of Ynez. He hummed to cover up the sound of the wall cracking. "Why people always disappointing?" Rockefeller moaned.

Pavel pounded the counter, shattering his mug. Tee went quiet. The bartender waved an imaginary paintbrush at the shards. Rockefeller said, "Katka," and what Tee seemed to recall were the words for *love* and *art*. Ynez reached for Tee's hand, but he shook her off and swept up the glass with a Staropramen coaster.

Pavel's eyes narrowed, and he dug a thumb into Tee's arm. "Is maybe good you go away," Pavel said. Tee stumbled, confused. He didn't yet know how resistance built up in Prague secret by secret, symbol by symbol. But he had noticed the calf slipping out the door. He sent Ynez home and returned to Karlín alone.

In Boston, when Tee woke from his flooded dreams, he would try to follow the ghost over that threshold into reality. He would try to remember when he had first seen the ghost. Was it that night, drinking with Pavel and Rockefeller and Ynez, but not Katka? Or was the ghost the same as the shadow in Pavel and Katka's house, the shadow he had seen from the closet?

After drinking in Vyšehrad, Tee woke to Rockefeller pounding his door. Pavel had gotten into a fight with a group of Americans. At the time, the ghost was quickly forgotten.

Tee had to imagine what happened. He didn't know for sure. Pavel and Rockefeller left Vyšehrad and gambled at a Herna bar in Malešice until four A.M. They crossed the street to the Flora mall, where they had chosen a storefront for their café, and balanced on the steps, in the dark, smoking. They spoke English—they liked then to practice running their tongues around the flat alien sounds in inflated iambs, as if each word were a stone. It was their third language after the Russian forced on them as children. Rockefeller blew out a long stream of smoke and said they would call the café "The Heavenly Café."

"I thought we calling it in Czech," Pavel slurred. He was having second thoughts about New York. He knew Katka was right: he should focus on his own country. He had the feeling that Tee was in love with his wife. It had just come to him, that night, watching Tee turn down Ynez.

That was when Rockefeller said Americans were the only ones who would buy Pavel's art now. Pavel tossed his cigarette down a grate and cursed. Once, Rockefeller had risked arrest to hang Pavel's art around Prague. As the sun rose, Pavel stumbled away from his friend. Over his shoulder, he called Rockefeller a *blbec*. It wasn't Rockefeller funding the café. Pavel walked down beside the Flora cemetery with his hands in his armpits and waited for Rockefeller to follow. A thin shadow stretched toward him—but not from behind, from out of the graves ahead.

Pavel wanted a fight. Urine gushed against a gravestone, and Pavel rushed in, shouting about respecting the dead. He must have seen only one American, not three. In the dark, in his drunkenness, was he fighting Rockefeller, or Tee, or himself?

The sun rose over the marble headstones. The three men surrounded him. A fist cracked his ribs. A fist hit him in the neck. Pavel screamed. He sobered immediately. He screamed his name, at first, hoping that they would recognize it or that Rockefeller would come. They shoved him onto a gravestone. When he tried to brace himself, his wrists struck hard. The first wrist, perhaps, broke then. On the ground, he screamed that he was a painter, as if realizing what he stood to lose. They beat him until he went quiet—or they heard him and his screams told them what to break.

He grabbed a leg and someone stomped his second wrist. He gave up and lay still. Only after the three men left him did Rockefeller step from the shadows. When the giant body approached, Pavel feared another attacker. He only recognized who it was as Rockefeller cradled him like a baby.

In September, in the hospital in Boston, when his parents' visits ended, Tee would sit in bed with a lap tray and an old automatic typewriter they'd brought him, and search the past. That attack on Pavel had led (somehow) to Rockefeller attacking Tee. Tee had found two rules to fates: one) if you hurt someone, that person will eventually find a way to hurt you back; and two) if you want anything, you have to hurt someone to get it.

One night Tee saw the ghost dart past his open door through the corridor to the bathroom. He pushed into the hall just in time to catch a ratty jean jacket and a black knee-length skirt, both unfamiliar. As he hurried after the woman, he could taste a change in the air, as if she had slipped a key under his tongue. The hall filled with rain. He tried to make the floor stay the floor. From somewhere he heard an instrument twanging—like the mouth harp his father had given him on his eighth birthday. But what he thought about was Katka and Ynez and Pavel and Rockefeller. *Who are you,* he asked in his head. *Let me see you.*

The bathroom was empty, except for him. In the mirror shone the five chicken-pox scars on his chest, the white bandage around his skull.

II

The morning of Pavel's attack, Tee took a taxi to the hospital. Katka met him in the hall. Her brown hair hung unbrushed, and she wore a black coat over a boxy dress. She took a step toward him, then stopped and wiped her hands on her coat. "He doesn't want to see you."

Tee's head split, a Red Sea of alcohol. "Rockefeller wouldn't tell me everything."

She said Rockefeller had hidden nearby and let Pavel get beaten.

"He said he couldn't do anything."

She stood just out of reach, shaking her head, yet waiting, as if to give Tee a chance to say something to bring her to his arms.

"It's not your fault," he said. "And it's not mine."

"I have got to take care of him," she said, "is what I have got to do now." She buttoned her coat as if suddenly cold and turned her tall figure down the hall with a sweep of her arm.

Tee started after her and called out, "I was wrong, in the closet." For a moment she put her palm to the wall, as if to brace herself, but she didn't turn back. He tried to speak so that she would understand what he meant. His voice cracked, and he couldn't find her scent in all the cleanliness. "I think maybe I don't have to close the door on myself.

It's like a revolution. You want a revolution to change things. But you really want it because it will make you more yourself."

"It is not a revolution," she murmured. She stepped into the room to her husband.

Tee slapped his hand against the wall, and his fingertips rang with pain.

In the corner of his eye, something moved. He remembered the calf the night before. He was about to follow what he had seen when a doctor walked up.

Tee asked about the artist's condition. The doctor pointed to his wrists. "Broke. Need surgery. How you know Pavel Picasso?"

"Will he paint again?" Tee asked.

"This injury"—the doctor tapped his head—"may be mental impact. Physical he will be okay. We fix him."

"Mental impact?"

"Mental," the doctor repeated.

Tee thanked him. Then he walked out through the white halls into the rain.

After the attack, Tee and Rockefeller were no longer welcome at the house in Malešice. Tee blamed himself: he had wanted them all to get drunk. He tried to visit, twice, but no one would let him inside. A policeman showed up at Tee's apartment to question him. Tee asked what the chances were of catching the attackers. "How you say it?" the policeman said. "Zero." Tee imagined American faces bearing down on the artist. More and more, he found himself across the hall or at the Globe. Rockefeller brooded, hunched into the collars of sports jackets. Tee asked about the flying horse on the bar sign in Vyšehrad: Šemik, Rockefeller said, that broke its leg jumping over a wall to save its master's life. Tee went by the Globe even when he wasn't on schedule.

Ynez joked that he had gone back to Boston to fall more in love with Prague. "It's not like you have to know what you're running away from," she teased, "to run away." Ever since that night of drinking, he had kept his relationship with her to the Globe. As if stepping outside would be more bad luck. He bought a book on the maidens' army, on the betrayals that led the sexes to war. He wrote myths in the margins of myths. In his, a version of him dammed up the Vltava, a boulder a day, rearranging the map of Prague. A version of him stomped on the hill Blaník to rouse its army of dead. A version of him broke into the Orloj and hung on the enormous gears until everything, everyone, slowed.

Ynez read over his shoulder. "Are you supposed to be Czech in these stories?" She chewed her pen. "Are those our books?"

"If I'm trying to run away from myself," he said, "can't you just let me?"

"Now who do you think I am?"

He slipped her pen cap into his pocket. When he didn't answer her, she said, "Where do pigs park? A porking lot."

He laughed and clutched at his chest.

"It's not that funny," she said. She narrowed her eyes. Finally she said, "What are you afraid of? Is this about your birth mother, your birth father?"

Tee raised a single eyebrow—his father's gesture, which Tee had copied, at first, because it made him look like a pirate. "What am I afraid of?" He told her how Pavel had stared at him that night, unblinking, before shattering the mug. He had stepped in front of her, Ynez, for fear not of Rockefeller but of Pavel. Ynez seemed confused why he should be afraid of the artist.

Tee remembered what Katka had said about lies. She had rubbed her nose and said, "This means you are telling the truth." Then she'd rubbed his. "Your nose is too soft," she'd said. "Do all Asians have soft noses?"

- - -

Pavel kept to his bed through most of May. The Globe filled with gossip. Rumor reported a successful surgery: two screws in each wrist, under twin casts. Tee imagined Pavel pulling up the blanket with his teeth, shivering like an addict. His fingers itching for a brush, his lips sucking for a cigarette. Each time Tee called the house in Malešice, Katka waited just long enough to know it was him before hanging up. Tee bought all the books he'd written in in the Globe and hid them under his bed.

The few expats the artist did allow over, Rockefeller invited to his apartment. He hosted dinner party after dinner party. The art dealer's daughter, Vanessa, said the bedroom studio was a mess of clothes, dishes. She'd seen an easel, in one corner, kicked in half. Pavel wouldn't let Katka touch it. Vanessa said she had lit cigarettes and placed them in his mouth; he'd nearly bitten her. She had gotten the feeling he wanted to. "Jára Cimrman lit his cigarettes with lightning," Tee said. No one mentioned the specifics of the attack.

In the Globe the staff sometimes went quiet when they saw Tee coming. Once, he overheard a woman with a book on Pavel's art say she was buying it because the artist was going crazy. Someone she knew in the Czech art world had gone by the house in Malešice, and Pavel had shouted for a full hour about certain young artists borrowing culture from the Americans, as if he blamed her friend and was about to stab him through the heart with a paintbrush. The cashier glanced in Tee's direction. But Tee knew Pavel couldn't lift a brush; that must have been embellishment. After the woman left, the cashier asked if Tee was okay, as if he was the one to be pitied, not Pavel. Ynez crept closer to hear his answer. Tee said the book the woman had bought was a good one.

- - -

One afternoon, while Tee killed time in an Internet café before work, he found an e-mail from his father. A link to a blog, of all things. *Finally in Hollywood*, his father wrote. *Apologies to my wife. Must get this film made or die trying. Heck, it's my best attempt to forgive myself.*

A couple of days later: *Had lunch with a film guy. I drew him a picture of my brother's crash. If only he knew everything I knew, he'd back this movie in a second. Why doesn't anyone see things as I see them? If you're out there, pray for me.*

Tee wondered if his father meant him, or maybe his uncle.

Finally Tee set a date with Ynez at the Cuban-Irish bar in New Town, O'Che's, where they stood no chance of running into Katka or Pavel or Rockefeller. They sat under the arched ceiling in the back, beside a stained-glass window of Che Guevara. Ynez asked what had taken so long; couldn't he tell she was waiting for him? He remembered his aunt and uncle babysitting once while his parents saw a movie. Half-asleep, he'd heard his aunt enter the master bedroom. Drawers squeaked open. Then his uncle's footsteps came upstairs, and the room quieted. Tee had tiptoed across the hall and heard the bed squeak. What had his aunt found that she'd tried to erase through sex?

In the bar, Tee noticed the noise of other Americans, the bravado. "I don't know what's wrong with me," he said, scratching the lip of the table. "You're right, I should have noticed."

Ynez said, "You're starting this date with 'It's not you, it's me'?"

He ordered shots of absinthe. *Just be a tourist*, he thought. *Someone who can take things or leave them.* Ynez modeled how to wet the sugar and light the spoon on fire, waiting out the flame before stirring sweet into the bitter licorice liquor.

The bar blurred at the edges. "Why did you choose this place?" she asked. "It's awful."

Outside, as they walked toward the night tram, he pulled her into him. She stumbled against his chest. A tenor sax whined over Wenceslas Square. It rained.

"For someone with a fear of abandonment," she said when he covered her with his body. Then she stopped, one heel catching against the cobblestone.

"Is that what I have?" he asked, his heart pounding.

In her bedroom he pressed his face between her breasts, breathing her in. He would not be his father, not drive people away and pretend he was the one who'd left. He didn't have anything to deny or atone for. But he kept premeditating his kisses. Beside her ear, under her chin, in the hollow of her throat.

She dug her nails into his back. "What are you staring at?"

She had a girlish room, unembarrassed by stuffed animals. He realized he was looking for the ghost.

"Fuck me," she said, surprising him.

He twisted awkwardly and slid off the bed. She sucked in a sharp breath. He bit his lips and felt for the pile of clothes with his foot in the darkened room. When she pulled the comforter over her head, he carried the pile into the bathroom.

He lay in his bed that night cursing himself.

The next day, Tee climbed over the railing in Vyšehrad and sat on the cliff above the Vltava. Sailboats struggled to tack against the wind. Back in the ruins, a little boy knelt in the prayer maze, eyes closed. When the boy left, Tee walked into the center. He found a tiny blue thimble, just big enough to catch a drop of rain.

III

The tree was a magnificent sugar maple at least a century old. "It makes the garden come together," Katka had said, meaning *garden* in the British sense. The maple reached up from the middle of the yard like a many-fingered hand beneath the green glove of leaves. It was weeks after Pavel's attack. A neighbor had called Rockefeller for help in the middle of a party, and all the guests had gone down to Malešice together. Katka balanced on a branch twenty feet above the ground, in the tree because of her husband.

Later she would tell Tee how Pavel had gotten the paintings out of the closet, somehow, and into the bedroom, how she had found him in the middle of them, as Tee had been months earlier. She had been cooking lunch. Pavel asked her to move his art into the kitchen. He often had strange requests for his work. She set the canvases in four rows, the painted sides to the wall, protected from the splattering gulaš. When she was done, he stood in front of her and kissed her.

Out of nowhere he lodged one cast against her chest, already holding her back, and with the other cast, he tipped the largest painting into the stove. When it caught fire, he kicked the canvases out of the house and into the wet grass. He was lucky he hadn't burned down the neighborhood.

Beneath the tree, Tee didn't know where to look: what was left of the paintings smoldered nearby; Katka's white limbs shone through the leaves as she swayed in the sway of the wind; Pavel yelled below, stomping in a bathrobe; the other guests pulled bottles from pockets and predicted a storm; the neighbor stepped back, rubbing his cheeks; Rockefeller yanked his jacket off his wide shoulders and beat at the dying flames. Tee guessed a storm would only affect Katka's grip. The art was beyond saving. The already damp ground had contained the blaze. The smoke itched in Tee's eyes, and when he wiped them clear, there was a second glow at the base of the tree. For a moment he thought he had been wrong and the tree was about to light up. But then the glow became a foot, as if the tree had flipped upside down and was about to walk away. Tee wiped his hands on his shorts and stepped forward, and the foot disappeared. Tee reached for the lowest branch, putting the ghost out of his mind. He swung a knee over. Katka waited in the middle of the branches, one place Pavel's casts could never reach her.

"How did you get so high?" Tee called up to her. "Are you okay?" Sap stuck to his skin. One off-move might send both of them falling. Her eyes shone clearly, even from fifteen feet above. She had tan shorts on, and her legs were scraped red by the bark.

Pavel circled the maple and yelled up in iambic English: "Stay out of it. It's privacy. I told you never coming back here." He tried to cross his arms, then remembered his casts and gave up. One of the guests asked if they should get a blanket for Katka to jump into. Pavel shouted that he would make Tee sorry. The wind carried his warning.

It was the first time since his uncle had died that Tee had felt the force of the wind. On the flight simulator on his parents' computer, he had nosed down again and again, never able to save himself. Katka wrapped herself completely around her branch, shivering.

Rockefeller stomped toward Pavel, and the two of them shouted in Czech, arguing or threatening. Their voices grew, then softened. Tee focused on the climb, shutting out everything else. "Hold on," he said. "I'll help you." He climbed another few branches before the voices drew back into the house. Maybe Rockefeller would get forgiveness after all, the thing he most wanted.

When Tee was four or five feet beneath her, Katka asked, "What do I mean to you, that you would climb up to me?"

He felt a strange mixture of anticipation and regret, as if the question of *meaning* was a mysterious box they'd been saving to open. *I want to know something about you that no one else knows*, she had said before she showed him the same paintings that now burned below them.

"Rain's coming," he said stupidly.

He managed to stand on his branch and get closer. The wind pulled at the threads of his balance. He waited for his container to give him weight, but he was light, emptying.

"He burned the paintings," she said, "and all I could say was 'fire.'"

Tee wrapped one arm around the trunk and pictured Pavel standing over the images of her, which he had made and then destroyed. Tee pictured Katka running past the fire to the tree, not knowing what she was doing. She hid herself where everyone could see her. Tee didn't want her to feel more exposed.

"Remember *The Giving Tree*?" she said. "I gave everything to Pavel."

"I'm sorry. I don't know where to begin."

"Do not say you are sorry. Do not ever be sorry. The thing about pity is you can never take it back."

"I wasn't pitying you." The sky seemed to close its jaws. Had she climbed the tree then because of that book? Once, while Pavel was painting in the bedroom, she had said that she *wanted* to love like the giving tree—without reservation. "Come down," Tee said, fumbling upward. "Things will change now."

She blinked and her eyes opened somehow bluer than before.

Below, a shout went up, and then Pavel sprinted across the lawn. Rockefeller close behind him. The air was full of static, like a TV channel had gone dead. Someone didn't want to watch anymore, Tee thought. Katka coughed, or stifled a hurt cry.

"Get out!" Pavel shouted as he ran toward them. "Get out of Prague!"

The sky dropped as if drawn to the smoke from the paintings.

Rockefeller reached forward. But at the crack of thunder, Pavel leapt and threw his back against the trunk. Tee held on as the tree shuddered. He heard the hiss of the fire as water washed down the bark. He looked for Katka. For an instant, he thought of Pavel's art, but it was black with ash, irrecoverable.

Katka shouted from her branch. Even in the chaos, Tee sensed she had more to say. He wished he could wait for her, forget the wind and the rain and the height. He wanted to listen without reservation. But he had lost his hold. Pavel and Rockefeller stood out like airbags, ten, eight, six feet below. Tee slammed into someone's shoulder, and they collapsed together, in a heap. Tee's ribs clanged like a bell. They lay on the grass, and the rain plunged into their eyes, tiny divers aiming for mistaken pools.

IV

The next day, Katka called to thank Tee for climbing after her. They met in a café in Karlín, an out-of-the-way basement Pavel and Rockefeller hated. A series of chambers extended underground. Tee dressed in a blue designer button-down, though with his usual khaki shorts and thong sandals. He wore the cologne his ex-girlfriend had given him, the only bottle he owned, though he didn't know if this was a good idea. He got to the café early. He wanted, for once, to be waiting for Katka. He ordered a Pilsner to calm his nerves. Fifteen minutes passed. She might have changed her mind. Someone stepped down the stairs, then turned on one glowing heel and headed back up. Tee sprang from his chair, spilling his beer, and went after. He poked his head into the higher chamber. He heard the bartender behind him shouting about foreigners. Katka was nowhere in sight. Tee crossed the chamber, and just as he wondered what he had seen, he nearly knocked her over—in a short blue summer dress, inches taller than him in her boots. They sat at a nearby table, and she ordered a glass of wine and he another beer. "How are you?" he asked. "Any better?"

"Better? I am not sure what you mean."

They sat for a while in the silence his question had raised. The waitress came, and he ordered a cheese platter.

"You did not answer me yesterday," she said finally, twisting the stem of her glass. "What do I mean to you? Why did you climb that tree?"

"I like you," he said. "I told you already. Why did you climb it?"

"Do you want me to say because of Pavel?"

Tee started to apologize.

"I told you," she said. "Do not be sorry." She took his hand, her skin unusually warm, as if she had been drinking already.

But he did need to hear about Pavel, for some reason. He didn't want to sound whiny, young, but he needed to know. His fingers, under hers, seemed bony and thin, as if his skin had grown transparent. Had his aunt seen through his father like this?

The waitress delivered their cheese, and before they ate, Tee clinked his glass to Katka's. Neither of them let their eyes drop. She'd told him that breaking eye contact while toasting meant bad intentions. "Tell me how you met," he said.

"Tell you how I met who?"

"You know who I mean." He tried to stop himself. He had seen that foot change direction, though, and he had to follow it to an end.

She drew a breath and seemed to decide. "After I graduated university," she said, "I ran messages for the artists and writers leading the protests. Pavel's father had just died in jail, and Rockefeller had printed their drawings side by side in a samizdat. I knew Rockefeller from when I was a girl, from before his family moved to Prague. His parents were important Communists, so no one suspected him, or they pretended they did not." Her other hand rubbed a stain on the table.

"He arranged a message. I took a letter to Pavel—that was how I met him. I believed in him then as an artist and a hero and a politician, though he only ever wanted to be one of those. I begged Rockefeller for the chance to meet him. I was like all the others: I listened to Plastic People of the Universe, I followed the news out of East Germany."

Three months before the Revolution, she said, she'd gone to Pavel's house and met a young man the same age as she, with shaggy hair and a jutting chin. He stood to the side and read suggestions from the artist Vašíček—she'd opened the letter out of curiosity—an old friend of his father's. He was stooped and timid at first, and she was disappointed. But once he finished reading, he said Vašíček's was an old aesthetic, and he wouldn't paint like his father. He would represent youth. As he ascended into surety, the fear she'd originally had, that she might embarrass herself before him in some way, pleasantly returned. His wiry frame seemed to grow sturdy before her, and when he asked her opinion of his art, her voice betrayed her. Only her body would react— she turned him around by the shoulder, so he couldn't see her. Then she pressed a single fingernail to the back of his T-shirt, and electric with boldness, wrote her name. He arched in a way that embarrassed her, though no one was around, and he spoke her name aloud.

"After we married," Katka said, "the May after the Revolution, he said I had hurt him that day. He said he had been afraid I would be able to do anything to him, and he would want it to happen. That was what we were like."

They had been Tee's age when they met. "Thank you for telling me," he managed.

"Sometimes you look at me like that."

In one of the oldest home videos of Tee's mother, she was washing dishes, and with each plate finished, she batted her eyes as if waiting for Tee's father to step out from behind and help her. After a few minutes she put down the sponge and pulled him in front of the lens and kissed him. Tee thought of that now, against his will.

"Why did you climb up to me?" Katka asked again.

"When I was a child," Tee said, "I was very sick once and almost died. In my sickness, I dreamed my dad took me to Manhattan and up to the roof of a skyscraper. He refused to wait in line for the Empire State Building. A woman rode the elevator all the way to the top with us, without talking, and when we got off, I held my dad's hand in fear. The wind blew so hard you could feel shapes in the shifting air, and I felt the woman run past us before I could see her face. She ran to the edge of the roof, and then she leapt off, arms out like she was diving into a pool." Tee tore off the top layer of his coaster. Katka wrinkled her eyes, confused, but she knew suicide.

"After I got better, I couldn't get the dream out of my head, it was so real. I bothered my dad until he agreed to a trip to New York. I don't know why he indulged me. In the end, after hours of walking, we found the same building, exactly as I had dreamed it, and we went up to the roof and the rooftop was the same, too, and I knew something had happened there. I'd known it all along. I'm not so easy to understand."

"You had a girlfriend," Katka asked after a pause, "in Boston?"

"There was a girl I thought loved me once. But she was just in my head."

"What do you call that? Puppy love?"

Katka finished her glass and the waitress came by. Tee's face was hot. He wondered what had made Katka mention her father so early on and then never again. As the waitress wrote down their orders, she stared at Tee; finally she asked if he was American.

"Truth?" she demanded when he nodded. He frowned and drank the rest of his beer. "You have phone call."

Katka pinged her wineglass with her fingernail. Tee hadn't told anyone where he was. She swept her hair over her ear and glared as he followed the waitress to the front desk.

Could he simply ignore the call? Maybe Ynez was in another chamber, hating him. Or Rockefeller had seen him leaving the apartment building and followed for some reason—but why phone? Maybe one of the regulars at Rockefeller's parties had spotted them and suspected something. Tee had nothing to hide.

"*Prosím,*" he said, picking up the phone.

"You said you wouldn't tell her about us," whined a woman with a New York accent.

"I'm sorry?"

"Come on, Tee, I saw you in there. You promised you wouldn't say anything."

"Vanessa?"

"Listen," Vanessa said.

"I'm not going to tell anyone about you and Rockefeller. Where are you?"

There was a pause, and then: "Then what are you two talking about, the day after she climbs a tree and her husband burns his art?"

"Good-bye, Vanessa," he said, and hung up.

He looked around but couldn't see her. There was no reception underground, which was probably why she hadn't called his cell phone. Rockefeller had trusted him with their secret relationship back in March. Vanessa had said her father hated her dating and would sell Pavel's art on eBay or something if he found out. The last of Pavel's unsold paintings, still intact, were at her father's apartment.

Back at the table, the drinks had arrived before Tee. He thought about what he could say to Katka, but she didn't ask. She wiped her lips and drained her second glass of red.

He shouldn't have hung up so abruptly. What would Pavel do if Vanessa told him she had seen Tee and Katka together, alone? Tee remembered the shattered mug, the night of the attack. That was nothing compared to what Pavel could be capable of now, an artist who would burn his own art.

Katka leaned toward him. The scent of cocoa butter. "Remember that day," Tee said, "in Vyšehrad, with the dogs? Pavel and Rockefeller appeared, and then you took off and pulled me along, and they ran after us. I didn't even know why we were running." Several dogs had jumped their leashes and joined the chase. Strange Prague everydays. "I've always been ready to follow you."

Her expression hardened. "Follow? Is that why you climbed the tree? That day in Vyšehrad, you rescued a girl no one else would, remember that? The dog had her in its jaws, and you let it snap at you so she could get free. Even her dad would not do that. On New Year's you seemed brave, going under the fireworks nude."

"Naked," he said. He remembered doing those things, only he hadn't seemed himself then.

"I had not thought you needed to follow," she said. "I thought you were more mature than your age, you were different than anyone else. You left your home behind. You left Korea. You left America."

People stared now, as her voice rose. And he was reminded, horrifyingly, of his mother. Like always: an Asian boy with an older white woman. Katka gripped his hands, and he wanted to let go, but he didn't.

She seemed to be accusing him. She brought his hands to her cheeks, as if he would slap her. "You're so young," she said, but she didn't look away. He knew by now that this was desire, an attempt to distance herself from what she wanted. She brushed his fingers over her lips. He knew what he'd agreed to by meeting her here, by climbing the maple. He leaned in and kissed her.

She shook him off and stood. "I have got to go," she said suddenly.

He shoved back his chair. Then he stepped in front of her, not caring who saw them, and kissed her again.

V

They got out of the cab in front of his building in Karlín, the rain coming on, and she said, "No one will know who we are. The rain will hide us." On the stairs, they shushed each other. They put their fingers to each other's lips. He went first to check that Rockefeller's door was closed. Then he waved her up. His heart thudded like a third pair of footsteps. He recalled what she'd told him about the truth, hard and soft cartilage. He rested his finger on her nose.

Wrong women. But he was defying, not repeating, the past. He touched Katka lightly on the arm, and she shivered. At the top of the stairs stood two ghostly feet. He stopped short. The feet didn't move. They weren't Rockefeller's. And Katka couldn't be in two places at once. Tee touched her arm again, solid and real. When he kept moving, the feet were no longer there.

In his bedroom, he whispered with a sharp ache, "This is right."

"No," she said, "promise me we will not pretend."

He pulled her toward him. He twisted her blouse in his fingers, and lifting it off, brought his darker skin to her lighter skin. He ignored the ghost passing his doorframe now. Katka moved his palms to her ribs, her breasts. He imagined his desire gathering her up, piece by piece. In her closet those pieces had been separate, a conspiracy of art. Now she was in his arms, whole. His fingers brushed the curve of her waist. Goose bumps rose on her cold chest. She kissed him harder, then softer, than before. He could hear the change in her breath. He bit her nipples, and she tugged his hair. He tried to make her same deep sounds, to hold nothing back. When she moved her mouth over his skin, she left cold, wet spots where her breath had been. She kissed his neck, he called her name, and she pulled him on top of her, locking her legs around the small of his back.

Afterward, they lay naked, staring out at the rain-scratched sky, hoping the storm would last. He traced a finger down her thigh, and she shuddered and said again, "Tell me something about you that no one else knows."

He opened his palm as if to wave hello. And then he knew what he could tell her.

"I heard my fortune once," he said, "after my Korean friend translated my birth mom's last words. My dad had said it was a name: *Kang Seul Peum*. But what it meant was 'river of sorrow.'"

He had left his friend with the words shattering in his lungs. "There was this restaurant in Chinatown someone had told me about, where a woman told the future. One look and you believed her. That woman said the break in my life line meant an early death or a coma, and my love line was so deep, I would never let anyone go." He brought Katka's fingers to his sternum.

"See these five scars on my chest? After the fortune-telling, I called my mom, remembering when I was six and almost died. Chicken pox and pneumonia. I had thought of my dad as saving me. A priest had come to say the last rites, and my dad stopped him. I guess I thought of it like adoption, a second time he kept me alive. But Mom said she was the one who made him go in that day, that Dad had thought I was a goner."

They made love again. The ghost stomped around in other rooms. He could hear it banging in his kitchen, but he didn't care.

VI

In the morning, Tee worked up the nerve to stop by the Globe. He'd been skipping his shifts. A man with horse teeth sat at Ynez's desk. The expats in Prague changed weekly.

"Tee," the man said—he was Irish.

"Do I know you?"

"I've heard of you. There aren't many Asians in Prague who come in here."

"I'm American."

The man winked. "Didn't know the word *Asian* would ruffle your feathers."

"Maybe you could take a message?" Tee had wanted to apologize to Ynez, but now he didn't know how. What message could he possibly leave?

"I heard you were with that artist the night he got beat," the man continued as if Tee hadn't spoken. "You and that big oafish lad who comes into the café, Rockefeller. Countrymen of yours, wasn't it? I hear that artist is plotting against you lads."

Later, Tee called back on his cell.

"You should talk to Ynez," a new voice said.

"I want to."

"Except she doesn't want to talk to you. She quit two days ago."

A cruel trick.

Tee wondered what Ynez had said when she left. He should have felt better to know that she was moving on.

After he hung up, he studied the objects in his dresser drawer: the blue thimble and the piece of the statue from Vyšehrad, the pewter Golem from the house in Malešice, the husk of the rocket from Old Town Square, the Pilsner and Budvar and Staropramen and Gambrinus and Krušovice coasters, two shot glasses, a few matchbooks, pencils and pens, stray buttons, an empty photo frame, a crumbling brick, a rabbit's foot from God knows where. Was this what he filled his container with? Or was it simple proof of where he'd been?

He spread the objects out on his bed. He remembered the shavings from his uncle's beard, the ash and bone in the urn. He remembered the Easter after he was accepted to Boston College, when his aunt had told him about her freshman year, the first time any of the adults in his family had ever talked openly about sex. Suddenly she had touched her cheek and said sex was all an act—she still dyed her hair every month, for men—and as she turned toward the living room, he was aware of a vulnerability he had never known before, in anyone. "All of this wanting and wanting," she'd said, nearly crying. "All of this not knowing what you want." At first he'd been embarrassed for her, trying so hard to connect with his youth when he couldn't help feeling put off by her sexuality. Later he'd been unable to shake the feeling that they had shared something, that she was keeping some secret for him, and he owed her.

In his bedroom in Karlín, Tee felt something, or someone, behind him, but he didn't turn around. He had locked his door. He picked up a red matchbook from Rockefeller's apartment. It advertised a Museum of Communism: PRAY WE DON'T CATCH YOU AT ANOTHER MUSEUM. Why would Rockefeller go there? Tee struck a match, and singed the edges of a piece of notepaper, as his mother had taught him to do once to impress a girl. Ash rubbed off on his fingertips, dusted the bed. What he was doing was not safe. He blew out the flame. In the center of the burned page, he sketched two eyes. He recalled the legend of Straba, who cut off the ears of his masked enemy, only to find, upon returning home, that the ears belonged to his wife.

That night before Katka arrived in the rain, Tee wrote in his notebook about Korea. As if telling her about the fortune in his palm had cleared up something about the past.

> *When Dad took the job in Pusan, he sent letters to Mom. He must have been trying to change. Soon, wasn't Mom sniffing the brown envelopes, imagining the Pusan beach and the hot springs beneath? But it wasn't long before the letters stopped. She would run at night, looking up at the windows and picturing windows in Korea. 2 months until he wrote again. Then the return address bore a hospital cross. She tore the envelope in her hurry, but he only had a broken leg. The end of his letter she reread again and again. He offered her what they had lost. A baby. When she called the number he'd given, what did she ask—why did he stop writing and where did he find a half-white baby? how much did he love her? did he already love the baby, me? He was in the hospital, had been in Korea just 6 months, after 2 quick trips to settle the contract. He said to make up her mind.*

VII

Over the last two weeks of July and the first two weeks of August, it would rain all but nine days. The storms would come and go, rarely lingering. The river would swell and rise up the embankments, but no one worried about a flood. Tee and Katka took no notice of warning signs, coming and going with the storms.

After they made love that first evening, he walked her down to Křižíkova station. He held a black umbrella over her and fought the guilt washing in in the wake of desire. They descended the escalators to the metro as a train rumbled by. The wind from the train stung Tee's eyes. Squinting, he saw a pink shape fly out of her hand and onto the tracks. She'd been holding her rain-soaked socks, and the wind had caught one. She'd let it go. Tee started after it, and a horn rang out. A second train flew up on the heels of the first, with closed doors, and after twenty seconds, went on.

"You looked like in your paintings," she said as the train departed, "rushing for a piece of clothing." She held the other sock behind her. The one on the tracks was gone.

"What are those ghost trains? I see them go by with their lights off and their doors shut." His ears buzzed with the rasp of the horn.

"They are for training drivers. Two people a month kill themselves in the metro. They step off the edge and get run over." He pictured this. Holding hands with her and stepping out over the tracks as a train crushed to a stop. "You have got to practice."

As they hugged good-bye, he knew that the next day would bring her back. He offered his umbrella, but she said she wouldn't be able to explain where it was from. He anticipated the next train, hoping for another dud. She plucked some wet fuzz off her shirt, and his hand went out to catch it.

"Do not worry," she said, and smiled. Then she reached out and pinched his wrist.

Later he realized she could have said she had bought the umbrella. Maybe she was afraid to have anything of his in her house.

Each time they saw each other, he would write about the stories she told him, about his family and hers, or about the ghost. On July 20, he wrote:

> I don't know why I agreed to see K only when it rains. It can hide us, she says. I wonder what Aunt A.'s excuse was for Uncle H. He pretended like there were two of her. Is that why I see a ghost?

Often they lay in bed and spoke of the chances of bad weather, staring up at the crests of paint on his ceiling. "Seventy percent tomorrow," Tee would say. They would make love until it looked like the rain was sputtering to a halt.

"Just stay over," he asked once, counting the time between thunder and lighting. Three, four, five.

"I do not know what Pavel would do to us." She put an earring—a gold apple—back into her ear.

Nine, ten.

The wind came down fast and hard and the rain drove at the buildings like tiny reckless cars. Sometimes he read to her what he wrote. She stretched across his blankets, long and gangly. He read her his fictionalized stories of her Czech grandfather and Roma grandmother, based on what she told him as she shared more of herself. He could never tell what she thought of his writing. She would hide her face as he read.

It is the early 1900s: Her grandmother gives up her tribe and the life of a gypsy contortionist to settle in Prague and have children. She speaks rapidly, expresses herself with her hands, brushes her hair over her ear when she's unsure. Her grandfather reads Kafka and Max Brod, writes unpublished novels.

Tee was translating them into the past. He understood this. Katka looked away. He didn't look away from her, or he would see the ghost.

"Is that right?" he said. "Tell me again?"

She shut her eyes as if the story lived just behind her eyelids. "When the Nazis were here, my granny had to deny she was Roma, and my mum and aunt learned to hate their past. My granny lost her identity—Mum said she became a vengeful woman who took out her loss on her children."

"And then?"

"When Communism took over after World War II, my family moved into the country. Mum came back during the Prague Spring. And she met my dad. He was a scientist—the borders were suddenly open, and he came to study our ecosystems. Mum was a student of literature; everyone liked her. They got married. Then the tanks trapped him. They fell in love in a time of freedom. They fell out after the Soviets invaded. Later, I suppose, they did not want to risk sneaking off to England with a baby."

She smoothed the pillow, the sheets. Finally she said, "I grew up a daddy's girl while he grew violent. Once, when I was seven, he slammed me against the wall. I had said we should escape together and leave Mum. Later that night he cried by my bed and said I was the one he really loved. I am sure Mum heard him. She is a stoic—is that the right word?—a sufferer who hears everything."

In a way, Tee thought, they'd both been left by a father, had left a mother.

Tee drew in his notes, in the margins of books, on coasters and napkins and peeled-off labels of beer bottles. People with children. Planes. Self-destruction. Whenever he noticed what he was drawing, he stopped himself. As soon as Katka arrived, he would cocoon himself in her visits. He had heard once that a caterpillar had to die in order to become a butterfly. A butterfly was an entirely new life.

When he asked about Pavel, about the state of her house, Katka never answered. Sometimes, after she left, he ran a finger over the pewter Golem he'd taken from her bedroom, as if it would grant a wish. For example: not to see the ghost, at least, when Katka and he were making love. According to legend, the Golem had been molded from the clay of the Vltava riverbanks. It wouldn't stop killing, so its creator had stopped it by rubbing out the word *truth* from its forehead.

July 29:

> *G'ma said it was like her two sons married versions*
> *of each other. Mom the quiet, tolerant girl; Auntie the*

restless, yearnful one. Each other's shadows. Doubled legends. A woman and a ghost. I have to stop this. Stop doubling the past with the present. They're two things in a line, not two versions of something else.

One evening when it didn't rain, Tee knocked on Rockefeller's door, and inside, he found Vanessa. She was a year older than he, an honest girl with a barely reserved mean streak. She had graduated from NYU and flown to Prague to assist her father. Rockefeller's hair stuck up in back, and the room stank of sweat. Vanessa lit a cigarette with a deliberate spark. What was Rockefeller trying to tell him . . . ? Tee didn't feel trusted now. He felt as if they had gone back to a time when one awkward visit meant your name on a list.

"How's life," Vanessa asked. Before he could answer, she pulled him into the hall, poked a finger into his chest, breathed smoke past his ear, and scowled. "What is your plan? To get with Picasso's wife? You're even more lost than I am."

Later Tee would wonder which afternoon Rockefeller found them out.

August 4:

Today I forgot to buy water and K mumbled to herself like Mom. Bit her teeth like Mom, too, that same click. Or did I imagine that? I remember, that time I got lost in Stop & Shop, I found Mom by that click. She was watching a man at the pay phone in front of her. She snapped her teeth together, and I heard it from all the way down the aisle. I couldn't call out to her, though. She had this sneakiness about her. When I got close, I knew why. The man at the phone was Dad. He didn't know she was there. She had forgotten I was there. "I hate you," she said under her breath. "I hate you. I hate you." And then, "I love you."

Tee would picture, later, Rockefeller walking across the street for a coffee, too lazy to take the metro to Flora where his own café was under construction. Maybe as he walked back, a woman ran out without an umbrella, and he thought he recognized her.

Or maybe he saw Katka as she arrived. A woman went up to the door ahead of him. He only recognized her when she stood too close to the building, which she did so that no one at their windows above could see her, or when she checked inside first before entering, or when she didn't look back to hold the door. Rockefeller paused then, not yet knowing why, before following a minute behind. In the stairwell, he heard sounds from Tee's apartment, a voice he knew.

For three straight days, it didn't rain. Tee drew Katka inside a raindrop. He worried about Pavel finding them out and burning the house this time. Tee took the coasters from the drawer and tossed them out the window like flying saucers. He slipped the Communism Museum matchbook back under Rockefeller's door, and left the rabbit's foot in an Internet café. The third night, he saw the ghost around every corner, always a step ahead of him. Katka herself was nowhere to be seen. He turned off the lights, and the sun behind the gray clouds outside seemed no brighter than the glow inside. The past—if that was what a ghost was, the past that haunted the present—should have stayed fixed as it was, suspended by time. But whenever he got near that glow, it was already coming from another room. When he couldn't take this game of tag anymore, he went to an Internet café and e-mailed his mother.

Tell me, are you happy now—divorced? I keep remembering the trip we all took together to the monuments in DC—I think I was 8? In the video Dad saved, we're like caricatures. Me a lovesick kid running to Dad or Uncle H. or Auntie only to return to you. Dad a lens on each of us just long enough not to seem pathetic. Uncle H. a soft-spoken vet who paid for everything as if embarrassed by $. Auntie, as soon as the attention left her, stuck in a mood, her color waning. You either pulling Dad or me aside or lingering at the back, always scarily aware.

I remember maybe 2/3 into the video, the shots got shorter. Dad was running out of film. He tried to conserve and kept missing the action. In the scene I can't forget, Auntie has a rubber egg from some novelty shop and is squeezing it behind you—did you know about this?—somehow so lewdly. "If I had a baby," she says to me. I take the egg from her and throw it down the street. When you kneel beside me, you tuck in my shirt but never ask why I did it.

I was always missing something. There was that day Dad took me to the library when he was supposed to be watching me at home. You came around your counter, as if you had expected us, and told Dad to go. He kept acting like he'd won something, but what? After he left, you put me in a corner with a book about geysers. Remember

*that? "Learn about your dad," you said. What was I
supposed to learn?*

I am serious. I am okay.

Love, Thomas

Maybe Rockefeller saw her on one of these days:

On the first, Katka stood at the kitchen counter, slipping mandarin slices into her mouth two at a time. She ate everything two bites at a time. "I know him again," she said. "He is painting again. He does not realize I am with you, because he is too busy thinking. He believes I am giving him time to paint."

"What do you do when he kisses you," Tee asked quietly.

"I make him believe I still want him. What else can I do?"

They made love that time too furiously, perhaps.

On the second, she said, "I think he has never done a better painting"—she was Pavel's subject again; he'd started to use the casts as brushes, started to return to art—"so how can he hate us?"

"How can he hate us?" Tee wondered how she could think their impact was less than it was. Less real than life.

Was that the time Rockefeller saw her, as Tee walked her out? *Promise me we will not pretend*, Tee had thought, shuttling her into the rain with an arm around her twitching shoulders. Three weeks and she had stopped taking her own advice.

VIII

These are the things Tee learned about Katka before the flood:

1. She ate well, a strong appetite always.
2. When she wasn't with Tee, she liked to go outside after dinner, briefly, for the changing light. Not to walk, though she liked walking. Not to garden, though she liked gardens. Sometimes, to stretch. She didn't like organized exercise, but she would exercise spontaneously.
3. Her father had studied butterflies. Her mother had studied literature.
4. She knew her neighbors, though they seemed surprised that she did, as if she was the type not to know.
5. She hated to lose. She was hardly ever jealous, but she was competitive. She avoided games. If she played games, she would exploit the rules ruthlessly.
6. Her puzzles were a way of recovering meaning. She enjoyed the work of physically rebuilding what her mind had already interpreted.

7. She could be simultaneously anxious and composed—
   her nervous tic was to brush her hair back over her ear,
   cleaning away her face.
8. She believed Hanuš had saved his clock, not destroyed it.

IX

Pavel was indeed painting again. He even invited Tee to see. "I had nothing to do with this," Katka said on the phone. On the tram to Malešice, a crowd got off in Náměstí Republiky and a leg glowed between them. Shouts carried from the square, but Tee didn't try to follow now. He went straight to Pavel and Katka's house, and Katka met him outside by the brown patch of earth where the paintings had burned. She warned him to be careful. She burrowed her heel into the patch and went to tussle his hair—he could tell—and stopped herself.

In the bedroom, Tee choked on dust. Pavel stepped down from a wooden chair. Behind him stood a giant canvas, eight feet high and four feet across, propped up against the bed. Tee wondered how they'd gotten it into the house. Bands of yellow, as wide as Pavel's casts, swept across the surface, one after another. The color bothered Tee. He recognized the curve: it was Katka, lying on her side. Katka again and again, slightly altered each time but always her. He could almost feel her hips. Pavel's casts were coated in yellow. The mess in the studio, if it had ever been there, was gone.

"You guess how I am doing it," Pavel said, waving his casts at Tee. "You guess."

Tee stepped backward, his stomach twisting. The casts couldn't create detail. What Tee saw was more like half a silhouette. Above were the ripples of yellow, tints from gold to dust, as if Pavel had dropped her in a yellow pond.

"It is his best," Katka said reluctantly.

Pavel wiped his casts on an already yellow towel and said he wanted Tee to talk to his dealer for him, instead of Rockefeller, about a new series. In the corner, a smaller canvas leaned against the wall, freckled by the same texture but a dark shadowy gray, a depiction of anger, or fear. It was as if Pavel had started painting himself and then switched to his wife.

"You wanted me to see a naked painting of Katka?" Tee asked.

Pavel's eyes narrowed and he sucked in his cheeks. Tee wanted to say more, but he was suddenly afraid, more afraid than he could explain. The yellow painting of Katka, the gray painting pushed to the corner. Tee leaned his shoulder against the wall. "This art," Pavel said, "is something new. Tell Rockefeller—how you say it?—he is dead to me."

Tee heard a faint grinding that seemed to come from the small, dark painting. Then he caught Pavel's jaw shifting back and forth, his earlobes wobbling.

When Tee got home that day, he had a voice-mail message. "Why don't you answer?" came his mother's voice. "You and your dad were always running or hiding from me." He pictured the expression where her face went from gentle to cutting in an instant, as if even her freckles rearranged. That look had cured him of his nail-biting, another of his father's habits. "Ignore that. I just wanted to hear your voice."

Tee's lights flickered, and in the dark, he remembered his mother hovering at his elbow when he was eight, as he held a homemade card over a candle for the first time. Halfway through, she snatched the card away, so that the last two edges burned more neatly. When Tee complained that the girl he liked would know he hadn't done those sides, his mother's eyes seemed to unfocus—as if she had another set behind the first, through which she really saw—and she said, "Because of these two sides, she will know you did some of it." As if mistakes were what people knew him by. He hadn't known how to undo her logic.

Was it that night, he wondered, the card tucked into his backpack, that she had determined he was too old for bedtime stories? She set a folding chair beside his bed instead of climbing in with him, and said it was time he read to her. He stumbled over words; she didn't correct him. She kneaded her palms as if she wanted to touch him but couldn't bring herself to. He wanted to tell her he loved her, but his voice was in her hands. When he woke in the middle of the night, the chair was still there, the lamp still glowed. He put a finger to the seat. It was warm.

He realized now: the glow of the candle flame, of the lamp, of Katka rippling through the painting, of the ghost that wouldn't leave him alone—somewhere in his mind, they were all the same.

Tee imagined Katka sprawled on the studio floor, nude and covered in dust. Pavel balanced on his chair above her and swiped his casts across the canvas. The bed propping up the painting stood in the middle of the room. They hadn't moved the bed in years. Underneath it, they'd found the layers of filth in which Katka now posed.

The dust itched; it stirred into the air; it made her cough. But Pavel painted a beauty she had never—even during the Revolution—seen in his art before. She modeled for him because she was cheating on him with Tee.

Pavel had been searching for undestroyed art and had reached under the bed with his cast. When his arm came out gray-yellow, he'd called to her, shouting dimensions. For his art, she'd bought the canvas and a dozen buckets of paint and batches of cheap towels. For his art, she'd cleared the room and pulled out the bed and set the open paint buckets around the chair and stacked the towels beside him, in two piles, one wet, one dry. To change colors, Pavel wiped his casts on a wet towel, then dried them, then, the space around his skin sealed with modeling clay, dipped his arm into a new bucket of paint, up to the elbow. She itched on the floor. At the end of each session, thirty towels went into the wash, gallons of yellowed water swirled down the drain into the Vltava.

In the evening after Tee had seen the painting, Katka arrived in the rain and they lay in bed talking. She told him how each time she posed and itched, she admired Pavel again. Though she longed to wash off the dust, then to let the rain wash her, then after meeting Tee, to wash again. Suddenly she was crying. He imagined the constant water meant baptism, meant forgiveness. Once, she had actually gotten off the metro to go back to Malešice, before a clap of thunder reminded her that Tee was counting the seconds. He didn't know how to respond to this—the ghost was about to appear, he could feel it. There were footsteps in the hall. He took Katka into his arms.

Tee imagined Katka watching Pavel climb onto a chair to work on the top of the canvas, jump down to work on the bottom. Pavel hadn't been this energized in a long time. He had grumbled and sat up in his sleep, panting, scraping his casts along the bed frame or the walls. Katka had asked him what would make him happy now. He'd rested his casts on her shoulders, one on either side of her neck. "If I found those Americans," he said. "I would kill them one by one."

X

The day before the flood, the day the ghost disappeared in Prague, not to reappear again until the hospital in Boston, Tee received the following e-mail from his mother:

> You asked if I am happy to be divorced. Well. I'm happy to stop pretending to be happy. I'm happy to stop waiting for your father to love only me. Can I give you some divorcée advice? Do not deny what you know. There is a reason I'm telling you this, of course—as there is a reason you asked. I must tell the whole truth before I stop myself. You have always asked to know more about yourself, I believe. You were curious about us, your dad and me, from the moment you could talk. You used to ask us, "Is Mom my real mom or is Dad my real dad?" as if one of us must be. You used to ask us to tell you the story of your adoption again, and I would listen to your father miss details he had given before. I remembered everything—you did too, then. You pointed out his errors! How could you forget that? Isn't memory a trespasser to

the heart? I have to admit, I've imagined telling you this many times. I used to ask your father, too. Ask why we didn't go through any adoption process. Ask why you looked so much like him. Ask and ask and already know the answer. Of course he was the same cheater in Korea as he was in America. He will always need other women. He will always hate himself. He will never satisfy whatever there is in him telling him he hasn't suffered enough. I'm sorry he, and later, I, pretended our secrets didn't affect you. I'm sorry I have to tell you like this, when I'm a little drunk. I'm sorry I didn't tell you before, when you and your father and I were all in the same house. But now that I'm divorced, and trying to be happy, I've realized—we need to know as much as we can about ourselves. You're your father's son, Tee. I mean his biological flesh and blood. You would have found out eventually.

CHAPTER 3
THE HUNDRED-YEAR
FLOOD: PAVEL AND
ROCKEFELLER

I

After his first week in Boston, Tee transferred to a rehabilitation center, a fat, low building like a hospital chopped in half. The inside like a retirement home. He would walk through the themed atriums at the end of each wing: rainforest, mountain, beach, jungle. Fake trees in brown cement. The staff ran a post office, a library, a restaurant, more for reorientation than utility. Twice a week an occupational therapist taught Tee life skills he'd never learned a first time, like how to tie your shoes so they never fall off, or how to speak to someone who holds power over you, or how to record dreams. He attended meetings more like support groups. Love was a common subject. A veteran with a re-aggravated head wound said they used to tell each other, "Cupid marches on." Hell or high water, Cupid marches on. In which war, he didn't say. A man who thought he was everyone's twin said, "So that's what I look like," and pawed Tee's face. "So sad."

At least once a week, in their meetings, one of the longer-term patients would urge self-forgiveness. Another patient always argued the value of regret. In their private sessions, Tee's OT spoke in metaphors, which she said patients could more easily understand. She said Tee was treating the past and the present like two magnets, forcing their ends together to see if they attracted or repelled. Tee said time seemed more like a house. He was in one room, a room that was the rehab center, and the room just next door was Prague. Of course, then he recalled what Pavel had said about shutting the door on himself. His OT asked him to tell her what day of the week it was. She hid the calendar behind her hand. He shook his head.

The way Tee wrote about Prague, it was like he was building that one room in the house of time. He started with a cobblestone floor. Then he added a golden roof, spires, an artist's canvas, books, a maple tree, water. But each time he built the room, it didn't seem right. How do you build in a ghost, or regret? He tore down the spires and the bookshelves and the fireworks and started over.

Tee's second night in the rehab center, he picked through a book he found in the library, on peaceful revolutions. The appendix had a page about Czechoslovakia. He wanted to imagine Pavel and Rockefeller overthrowing Communism, together, without violence.

The start of the Revolution, November 17, 1989, International Students' Day, was also an important day to Pavel and Rockefeller's relationship. They had joined twenty thousand Czechs and Slovaks, students with banners and flowers, in a march against Communism. Riot police cut off the marchers in Národní Třída, cordoning the square. The sudden panic squeezed Pavel between parked cars, away from Rockefeller. He wished Katka was beside him, but she had stayed home sick.

The police advanced, truncheons swinging. People sat, in protest, or tried and failed to run. Pavel searched for Rockefeller's mop of brown hair above the other heads. A man rushed past, in the direction they had come, holding his mouth. Teeth dropped like coins at his feet. A woman tried to escape down a guarded alley, and a policeman smashed her between the shoulder blades. A sharp pain bloomed in Pavel's neck—an elbow, or a fist—and with it sprang the smell of vomit, as if the bloom had traveled from his neck to his nose. A pair of arms wrapped around him from behind, and when he tried to shake them off, the flat of a bone in his back shoved him forward.

He almost fell, struggling against the crowd, before he heard the familiar voice in his ear. Rockefeller helped him onto a hood. Rockefeller steadied him with one big arm, kept people away with the other. Some student in the crowd recognized Pavel and she chanted his nickname, like a war cry. The chant got louder and louder—to Pavel's surprise, part of the crowd joined her. "See a way out?" Rockefeller said, shaking him. Pavel searched, as the car rocked beneath him, until he spotted a woman slip out down a side street, unharmed.

He shouted over his name. A harelipped boy climbed the car as Rockefeller tugged Pavel down. Metal scraped Pavel's skin, and he stepped on an arm or a leg. Rockefeller swam through bodies, chanting with the others now. Around them rose the scent of blood and bile and crushed petals.

At the alley Rockefeller towered over two short guards.

In the rehabilitation center in Boston, Tee wrote a room for the Velvet Revolution. In that room was Pavel's belief that Rockefeller would always help him. On the walls hung two paintings, one for each time the Secret Police abducted Pavel's father—after the second time ended in death, in 1987, Rockefeller had tracked down anyone still hiding the older artist's paintings in their homes, and had returned the art to Pavel. Fifteen years later Rockefeller stood by as Pavel's wrists were broken.

A month after Czechoslovakia became a democracy, Pavel and Katka married and Rockefeller started the first of six failed businesses, with revenue from Pavel's museum sales. The rest of their friends moved on with their lives. The more the world moved on, the more Pavel and Rockefeller clung to each other. To the two of them, Pavel's art was still an active influence, Rockefeller was still a force for change. They were each other's best reminders of their own importance. They must have come to resent how much they relied on each other, and the nagging sense that alone, they, too, would have been able to move on.

Tee touched the bandage around his skull. His fingers smelled like gauze. He put the typewriter away for the night. Before he fell asleep, the ghost woman glowed past his door. In the dark, Tee's hand crept to the typewriter paper. He wanted to get out of bed and give chase, or at least write another room, but he was heavy with sleep. A few minutes later, he was dreaming of Katka in the flood.

In the morning, he returned the library book. As he stepped into the hall, the ghostly leg turned a corner in front of him. He ran after it, though his balance had barely improved. He could smell the difference in the halls: water. Then he slipped into someone's arms, never touching ground. *Wake up*, he thought, *you're still asleep*. Nothing happened. The arms were real. He panicked at first that it was Rockefeller, until he heard the nurse's voice. She asked if he was okay. His father had called to say that he would be late. Tee reset his feet. He didn't want to lose the ghost this time—he felt as if those arms around his chest might erase the ghost's existence. But the next day, the calf again passed by his room. What had made it disappear in Prague? What had made it come back? If he caught it, could he return to who he was?

Tee didn't know. He imagined and imagined.

II

Pavel stood in the mud outside his house, in his bathrobe. Rain dripped down his casts. The gap was wider than a month before; his forearms had thinned. He searched for Katka in the distance, for a figure fading into the early-morning rain, but saw nothing. She had left him to go to Tee.

His wife.

They had fought the entire day—how terribly short a day was— and into the night. He wished, at least, that he could stop thinking of her as art. She had called him controlling, and her words had splashed bright yellows and reds, then dark blues and grays. He had always known the dramatic moments of his life as paintings. But at the end, he had wanted her to stay skin and bones. His wife. The woman who had slept with him, talked with him, hurt him.

She had left him for a foreign, dark-skinned boy, whom Pavel had given shape, color, texture. Pavel had burned her shape, color, texture. Was that why she'd left? She had begun to waver—when? As soon as they saw Tee stripped to his boxers in Old Town Square, under the fireworks? Or the morning she appeared in the hospital room, her blue eyes darting to Pavel's bruised, swollen wrists? Near the end of their fight, he'd said she was always a gypsy, stealing a heart and fleeing. He had been sure that would sting enough to give her pause, but she had lowered her voice and said Tee would never say that.

Maybe Pavel should have taken her hand, gotten down on his knees and begged. The affair with the American could never last. Later she would want her marriage back, but how could Pavel accept her again? At least if she hadn't told him she was cheating, he wouldn't hate her. Grief would be better.

Just before she left, she said it would be okay. A stack of dishes sat on the counter, and before he knew what he was doing, he had swept a cast into them and knocked them to the floor. Ceramic flew everywhere. Her hand darted to her calf. But then she simply wiped off the blood, pulled on her boots, and towered over him. "You had to turn violent," she said, "in the end?"

He'd said, "If we divorce, you'll get nothing, since you're at fault." She'd said now she knew what kind of person he was. He'd said, "I'll find you and get you back if it's the last thing I do." She'd said, "You really think I would get back together with someone like that?" She'd thought about getting back together. He'd made himself easier to dismiss.

He plunked out into the muddy yard. He pushed down one bare foot as hard as he could, as if to be sure he left a mark. The rain washed over the city, dirtying and distorting. The prints of Katka's boots already faded in front of him. She had bought those boots after publishing a single art review, in a British magazine—the only money she ever made in her life. Maybe she'd planned ahead for this day. Under the mud was the charred grass where he'd kicked out the burning paintings. He dipped his casts into the mud until they were browner than Tee's skin, and then he slammed them together. He clutched the casts tight to his chest, in pain. On an impulse, he pressed his lips to one cast, extended the tip of his tongue to the mud, and swallowed.

III

A week before the flood, Rockefeller had gone to Vanessa's father's flat to discuss the gallery in New York. Vanessa was the only one there. They'd started fooling around on the sofa, his pants thrown off and her skirt hiked up. That was how her father found them. Rockefeller saw the threat in the man's curled lips, in his wide white teeth. Then it was simple instinct: in an instant he had one big arm against her father's throat. He asked where Pavel's paintings were. He had to save them. He would sell them himself or find another dealer.

Vanessa tugged at his elbow. He realized they must have been reckless on purpose. They must have both wanted to see what they would do if her father caught them. He didn't feel bad about this. What he felt bad about was that for a moment, he kept pressing the bulge of her father's Adam's apple.

A few days later, Rockefeller asked Tee to come to The Heavenly Café—the name-to-be stenciled in black on the café windows, white sheets covering the glass from the inside, islands of concrete slabs and two-by-fours and scrap metal sticking up from the floor. Without Pavel's money, the construction was on hold. Rockefeller kept listing his past business failures in his head: newspaper, gallery, bookstore, radio program, real estate, city tour.

Tee arrived full of confrontation. "I saw Vanessa the other day," he said. "She said you guys broke up and Pavel's deal is off? What the hell?" He closed his hands in his armpits, as if mocking Pavel. He didn't seem to notice what he was doing.

Rockefeller pointed to the four paintings against the back wall. "You listen," he said. The paintings of Tee were the last of Pavel Picasso's unsold art. Rockefeller pulled Tee through the rubble until they were almost touching the canvases. "I could tell Pavel your affair, that you with Katka . . ."

Tee started to back away. Rockefeller held him gently but firmly. He could still feel the arch of Vanessa's father's throat.

A moment passed, and then Tee mumbled, "Why do you have those?" He reached for a canvas. Rockefeller knocked his hand away. "If you still want me to invest," Tee said quickly, "I'll give you whatever you want. Just don't act like I'm the only guilty one."

Rockefeller had considered Tee's bribe, the café still a purgatory. Without more money, there would be no whine of cappuccino machines, no rustle of pages, no clink of cups on saucers, no conversation. The only options were to take Tee's investment or to tell Pavel about the affair and hope that won back the artist's trust.

Early the first morning of the flood, Rockefeller shifted his attention between his TV and the dark windows until the announcement that Karlín would be evacuated. On the news a scientist scratched his ear and said floods of this magnitude hit once every hundred years, and they were due. The scientist didn't expect the rain to stop, or the river to stop rising, for days. Other cities had already flooded; the debris was washing downriver into levees. It would break into Prague with enough force to smash windows or kill waders trying to escape. A city official warned that the floodwater would rise through the sewage system and infect open wounds, cause serious illness if swallowed in excess. The water level would reach five to ten meters.

Rockefeller went across the hall to warn Tee.

Rockefeller could imagine the flood washing Tee out of Prague, the affair ended, Pavel saved from that pain—but then he would have no café.

When the door opened, Rockefeller stepped in ready to shake hands. In a few hours the sun would rise and Karlín would be underwater. Tee probably had no idea. Other expats had called earlier, seeking translation. They could go to the café together, revisit the blueprint Rockefeller had lost, make the best of things. He had Pavel's art, Tee's investment.

But there was Katka, soaking wet, at night and not with Pavel.

Rockefeller's hand drew up as if reaching for a balloon that suddenly floated away. Katka stepped behind Tee. Rockefeller's mind raced: she must have left Pavel. She stared at the floor, twisting her rain-dark hair over her ears with both hands. Her fingers netted at the back of her neck so her elbows stuck out like wings.

"We all must go," Rockefeller said when he could speak. "The flood is coming. Karlín soon will underwater."

"Flood?" Tee said. "What are you talking about?"

"Get out," Rockefeller said. "You must go now." He pushed other words back down into his lungs, and then he was whispering in Czech: *Aren't you ashamed?* He straightened to his entire height.

Katka's eyes flashed as blue as if the ground had blinked open to an underground river. Rockefeller turned, for a moment embarrassed. When he looked back, she had disappeared into another room.

His hands squeezed into fists, the balloon back in his grasp. "Forget it," he called in Czech. "I didn't see you."

Tee glanced around. Rockefeller had to get the money now—before it could be withdrawn, the affair out in the open. His palm itched. An old proverb predicted violence. But as his breaths quickened, shallowed, he stepped back and closed the door behind him.

Outside, he imagined them in there. Those dark hands on that light face. Sweat beading on Tee's forehead, Katka's fingers in his black hair. Rockefeller sent Tee a text: *Send her to husband.* He hefted the phone like a rock meant for a window. Hours later, in Old Town, he would receive Tee's reply: *She has left him for good.*

Rockefeller returned to his apartment to pack. He found the old camping bag he'd taken on kayak trips downriver from Český Krumlov, with Pavel and Katka and their other friends from the old days, since lost. Pavel and Katka had once seemed an ideal. At their wedding reception, Pavel had stolen his wife away from their party, and when they returned, all the guests had gotten him to bend down and propose again, as if they could have the day twice. The morning after, Rockefeller had even proposed to the bridesmaid beside him.

Into the bag Rockefeller put his father's collection of beer steins, the box of photos he'd long stopped adding to, the deed to The Heavenly Café. The radio repeated the evacuation orders. Rockefeller gripped his father's favorite stein, made by a glassblower who'd turned out to be Secret Police, turning the glass over in his hand. He wondered where his parents were, in a cabin in the Alps perhaps, his father learning to ski, coming home from the mountains to his mother's cooking. He imagined they thought of themselves as retired, too proud to work or to write to him, too proud to forgive their son for sending them away instead of trying to get them pardoned. Rockefeller had hoarded his connections, writing the names of people who owed him favors in a tiny brown notebook, only to lose those favors over time. At least he'd made his parents leave before they were arrested.

When he opened the box of photos to a picture of Pavel and Katka and him, on top, Rockefeller emptied the bag and packed survival gear instead. Tins of food, the bottles of water lying around in case of hangovers, extra pairs of shoes, clothing, a towel, bandages, first aid equipment. Out there, people would need help.

Then Rockefeller realized that with Katka gone, Pavel would need him, too, would need his last good friend to make him less alone. Maybe need Rockefeller enough to forgive. Rockefeller slung the bag over his shoulder and took an umbrella from the closet. He felt certain he would see Pavel before the flood ended. At the last moment, he repacked the deed to The Heavenly Café. Just in case. A streak of dark blue light loped along the sky's border. He imagined Katka inside Tee's apartment: saying, "I do not care about Pavel anymore," saying, "Pavel does not care about me, only art," in English, while Tee touched her greedily. But she had fallen for Pavel's paintings and ideas, things Tee could never give her.

IV

In the morning, the rain still pelting down, Katka still gone, Pavel stood before his latest painting. He dripped on the hardwood floor. He listened to the slaps of the rain, and then he bent to the modeling clay, and with his teeth, worked the clay into the space between his casts and his wrists. The sour taste made him gag. He stepped onto the chair in front of the canvas, then dipped his arm into a bucket of yellow paint. He raised that cast above the curves of Katka's body, the speckles made by the rough texture of the plaster, intimating dust—but he couldn't destroy it. In that moment, he didn't believe their marriage was over. He got out of that room, where Katka had lain naked, on the bed, in the dust, and he collapsed on their sofa, numb. With the point of his elbow, he switched on the TV, for the sound, any sound.

What he found was the flood. Immediately he hoped Tee would protect her and get her home. Then he banged his cheeks with his casts. He couldn't even wipe his tears. There was no way he could let Tee get away with this. But how to stop the boy? Become like the Secret Police, drag him away in the night? On the TV, helicopters followed the river washing over sandbags into lower-lying streets. A cyclist sped out, water splashing his waist. The news said the flood carried sewage—Pavel would remember that, later. He fumbled the phone off its hook and, with a fingertip, dialed Katka. He bent his ear to the receiver. She'd turned off her mobile.

The news showed workers evacuating animals from the zoo on Císařský Island, in the north of Prague; a hippo dangled from a crane, black rubber wrapped around its belly. A zoo worker discussed where the animals would go, how they might handle the stress. The news showed water full of debris, furniture smashing bridges, wood paneling splintering into dangerous shards. An architect and a former construction worker talked about faulty bricks.

Pavel bit the clay out of his casts and dialed a taxi. He was crossing the city, from one image of his wife to another. He had to show her he could save her. Once, she'd believed he could save the country.

When the taxi pulled up, he was struggling with his clothes. He shouted for the driver to wait. He inched his sweatpants up his thighs, using the friction of his casts. The cab honked, twice. Pavel knocked his wallet over, squeezed some money between his wrists, and left the house as the car pulled away.

After calling another taxi company, he waited outside, wet and cursing. When the second car came, he knocked a cast against the handle until the driver understood. Though how was he to rescue anyone when he couldn't open a door?

They drove north through Malešice toward the river valley. As they drew closer, the smell of dirty water made Pavel cough. He tried to remember what the news had said about the evacuation, but then the police blocked them off from Karlín. "That's it," the driver said. "We can't go any farther."

"You've got to be kidding me," Pavel said. "What are you getting paid for?"

"Excuse me?"

The cab screeched to a stop. Pavel fumed. But he didn't say another word. He knew about the taxi gangs that sometimes formed.

In the street a young policeman looked Pavel over, wet sweatpants to wet casts. They had been sized up like this at anti-Communist rallies. "My wife is in there," Pavel said.

"No one is in there," the policeman said. "Everyone's been evacuated."

Pavel imagined the water creeping toward them, the buses headed out a different way, the flood carrying the bodies of people who ignored orders.

"This area will soon be underwater, too. Unless you've got a boat, you're not going anywhere."

Pavel tapped his painted casts together. "I'm Pavel Picasso," he said.

The policeman laughed. "Do you have a boat, Picasso?"

V

Once, during the Revolution, Rockefeller and Katka had gone to a demonstration ahead of Pavel and had distributed his anti-Communist drawings on broadsides. People happily took them, but Rockefeller grew bored. Some of the protest leaders prepared to speak. Rockefeller said they should speak, too—he could get them on stage—but Katka refused, surprising him. He handed her the rest of the copies, letting go too quickly. As the broadsides spilled to the ground, she stooped and retrieved them. He hurried forward.

He remembered this now as a policeman walked an old woman toward a bus. "What will I do when I get back?" the woman said. "My nurse will come tomorrow and think my family took me." The policeman led her by the arm. "I came to this building to die."

Rockefeller started after them, but another policeman turned him around by the elbow. "Is there anyone else in your building?" the policeman asked.

"Tell that woman everyone knows about the evacuation," Rockefeller said. "Tell her that her family will know she is fine."

The policeman cocked his head. "Who are you?"

Rockefeller remembered how they'd acted under Communism, when no one knew who was Secret Police and who wasn't. "Do it," he said, and rushed off to help others.

He turned back once—the policeman was trying to find the right woman.

As he hurried west toward Old Town, Rockefeller pressed apartment buzzers and shouted into intercoms; he carried children to buses in one arm, and held his umbrella over them with the other. People stopped to ask about the flood, or to share news. "They say a tidal wave is coming," a man told him. "A small tidal wave."

A boy ran after his father with a dog in his arms. "Look at these scratches," a woman said, revealing the tops of her breasts. "My cat refused to leave. I knew something was happening when she stayed up on a bookcase all yesterday. I think the scratches are infected." Another woman said the police had forced her to leave her husband; he was sick and had kicked and screamed as they tried to get him out. "He'll outlast them," she said. An old man asked where he was supposed to go; he hadn't left Karlín in two years and had forgotten the rest of the city. A boy waving a foam sword said the military was going to bomb a ship that might sweep downriver and destroy the Charles Bridge.

Rockefeller directed tourists to trams, told people which parts of the city the news had said would be hit worst. Karlín, the Lesser Quarter, the Jewish Quarter, Old Town: the one, new; the other three, centuries old. A few people railed against him, said to leave them alone, it wasn't his place. They knew somehow that he had no official role. A few turned and asked advice of others.

Rockefeller wandered down to the river. A metal barrier had been put up along the embankments through Old Town to the Bridge of Legions. The Charles Bridge stood ready to prove an old myth that egg yolks mixed into its mortar meant it would never fall. Legends of Prague fluttered on the lips of evacuees as if to remind everyone of how long the city had existed, but Rockefeller didn't trust legends. In the

Jewish Quarter, a man reenacted King Canute's prayers for the river to retreat, courting laughs. Tee would have laughed. Rockefeller wondered where Katka and Tee would go to escape. For the second time that day, he nearly wished the flood would get rid of them, leave Pavel to mourn and move on—not doubt, wonder, self-destruct. Rockefeller imagined them on a bus, flipping over in a sudden increase of water. He imagined them hit in the head by flotsam, drowning slowly in a freak accident, one of the military's bombs gone wrong.

If they survived the flood, maybe Pavel would find his old nerve. Once, a man had insulted his father's art and Pavel had planned revenge for six months.

Rockefeller passed long lines at ATMs as if cash would solve everything. At one, a man pushed forward. A woman fell to the ground, and Rockefeller was upon him. "What are you doing!" he said. His bag swung down on his arm.

The man shrank backward. "An accident. An accident."

Rockefeller bent over him, but something touched his ankle. "Please," the woman said, "just leave us alone." She trembled. The man shook his head like he didn't know her.

When he left them there, he felt as if they'd said, as his headmaster had said during a school commemoration of Lenin, that he was too stupid to understand.

The barriers stopped at the Charles Bridge. Food, clothing, furniture, trash, parts of poorly built houses, even a few casually dressed mannequins, swept down the Vltava. A clutch of tourists lined the banks. The water almost reached their feet; the bridge's arches were submerged. Rockefeller's face was wet. He must have left his umbrella near the ATM. An explosion rang out upriver, and heads turned. The water smelled strongly now of garbage and sewage, dredged-up filth. The flood covered the islands: he could barely see the top of the museum on Kampa. More explosions sounded. Tourists snapped photos and talked into cell phones. Ambulance workers ferried people across to the Lesser Quarter.

At the hospital, after Pavel's attack, the doctors had asked Rockefeller questions he didn't want to answer, like what exactly he had seen. When he told them Pavel's name, they called colleagues. We can save his career, they seemed to tell each other. They put his wrists back together. But by that time, Pavel had told security to keep Rockefeller away.

Where were their old friends now, and the foreigners Rockefeller had invited over after Pavel's attack? Where was Vanessa? She had her father to look after her.

Rockefeller crossed the Bridge of Legions into the Lesser Quarter, dripping rain. Along Smetano Nábřezi, a crowd gathered clothes washed downstream from a department store. They wrestled over outfits. A woman shoved a boy away from the river. When he saw Rockefeller, he said, "It's not fair." Rockefeller unzipped his bag. He wasn't sure what he could give the boy, but as soon as the bag was open, the boy ran off with an old pair of shoes far too big for his feet.

The fringes of the crowd turned to Rockefeller, reaching. Rockefeller wished to lead by example. He widened the opening. A wet man took the towel to wipe his forehead. A man with a gash on his arm swiped bandages. And then they were taking anything. As a man pulled the bag away, Rockefeller remembered the deed. He pushed through the crowd. He tore back the bag, and the man stumbled with the force of the movement and fell. Rockefeller shoved his hand inside. "Where is it?" he asked.

"I didn't get anything," the man said from the ground, the rain sputtering down on him. The crowd followed.

Rockefeller flung apart the man's wet hands. Nothing. He carried the bag away from the river, and shook it out. Gauze and a bottle of water dropped in the mud. The deed floated down on top. He closed his fist around the paper and stuffed it in his pocket.

"I wasn't trying to steal from you," the man whined. Rockefeller walked past toward the road.

When he could think clearly again, reject the image of another crumpled body, Rockefeller returned to the swollen river. He tried to light a cigarette beside the stretch of land that usually formed a bridge to Kampa Island. An empty refrigerator smashed against the side of the museum. A floral-patterned couch scraped up along what was now the shore, at his feet. He smoothed back his wet hair and threw the cigarette on the ground.

A white face rushed downriver, a white shirt like a flag—and Rockefeller dove into the water. The body caught on some underwater crag. Rockefeller fought forward, churning his arms. The river pushed against him. Finally he drew even. So awkwardly stiff: a mannequin.

He held the mannequin in his arms anyway. He steadied his feet in the current, and threw the body ashore. When a female model followed, he threw her onto land as well. He waded back and lay beside them, the two plastic people dripping with rain and floodwater. Sewage residue stuck to them and to him. He swept a finger under his waistband, wiped off the sludge with the camping bag, and retched.

As he lay on his back, a memory flitted in undesired of the first brave thing he'd ever done, skipping a workers' holiday in secondary school. His teacher had filed a report about his attitude that might have damaged his family's reputation. His parents had been forced to use up a favor to get someone to "lose" the report.

He had only been showing off. He knew his parents would come to his rescue.

He stuffed the mannequins under his arms, the man on his right, the woman on his left, and crossed back over the Bridge of Legions toward Karlovo Náměstí. Almost no one was out, except along the river, and the wide absence in the streets seemed the aftermath, not the beginning, of disaster.

VI

It was evening when Pavel walked into The Heavenly Café. The stink of the river rose in his throat. Two mannequins dripped brown water. Rockefeller drank coffee and circled them, a male and a female. Pavel rubbed his casts on his shirt, streaking it with mud, without noticing. Four canvases tilted against the back wall. Pavel pushed past a pile of concrete and, with his casts, tried to slide the frames, the last of the paintings he hadn't burned, images of the boy his wife loved, through the mess. He couldn't concentrate. Back in June, Katka had painted him for once, turning the tables. He thought of that now.

She put the brush to the canvas, something he could no longer manage. He settled, naturally, into a pose. He even gave some instruction—how to see shadows, how to see what didn't want to be seen—knowledge he had saved up over the years. She had studied art in college, but when she turned the canvas around, it was the simplest insult. A paintbrush erect from his crotch. "Maybe you were always like this," she'd said, "but this is what I see now."

He couldn't let Americans take both his wrists and his marriage. He wanted an equal revenge—Rockefeller's wrists broken, his wife brokenhearted, Tee permanently alone. The sound of the rain came from far away. In the rubble in front of Pavel, Rockefeller lowered himself to his knees. His thighs shook, and he hung his head. His hair poufed like a wet bird.

"I'm sorry. I have to tell you something. I saw her with Tee."

Pavel hooked his fingertips around a painting.

"They're in his apartment."

Rockefeller rose and pulled Pavel's cast away from the painting. He drew out a pack of Marlboros. Pavel sat on a slab of concrete. Rockefeller started two cigarettes and held one between them. Then, remembering, he slipped it directly into Pavel's mouth. Pavel breathed in. His stomach was empty. It had been days since he'd last smoked. His arms and legs tingled. On the blank back wall, an image started to come to him.

VII

They moved around the café together and rearranged things, searching the slabs of rock and wood for the musculature of a business. Rockefeller stood the mannequins near the window, and Pavel gave them names, Petr and Petra. Pavel turned their backs to each other, slid them in close to kissing, bent an arm to a waist in a way that could have been reaching or pushing.

After a while, Pavel said, "You must do this for me. Get the buckets of paint in my house. Get the towels. Get the clay. Get everything. And promise you'll help me get her away from Tee."

In the house in Malešice, Rockefeller found the wreckage of a fight: broken dishes, running water, displaced furniture, scattered clothes. Against the bed leaned a giant canvas. Pavel had mentioned he was painting with his casts. Wide yellow swerves layered one upon another. It was hard to make out shapes or meaning. Rockefeller tried not to care whether or not this painting could convince anyone of a revolution.

He rested an umbrella from the house in the crook of his neck and carried the equipment to the café in several trips. On the second trip, he stumbled on the wet cobblestone and dented a bucket, but the lid held. He pictured himself paint-splashed in the middle of a flood. He tried not to hurry. Sirens wailed, deeper in the city. The rain poured down and he tucked the towels under his jacket. His teeth chattered, though he wasn't cold.

When Pavel had his supplies, he stood on a ladder and painted a mural over the entire back wall of the café. Those same thick swerves. Rockefeller toweled off the casts and held up buckets of different colors. This was what Katka must have done. She must have hoped, as the guilt from sleeping with Tee ate at her, that Pavel would paint himself back to self-reliance. If they were lucky, the mural could get on the news. Rockefeller still had a few favors he could call in.

"Promise me," Pavel said. And Rockefeller agreed. He had to know that Pavel forgave him for the attack. "I will paint for you. You must do what you see."

Along the river, the flood continued. Pavel asked for the radio. Zoo workers euthanized an elephant that might otherwise have rampaged in through the city. Someone got injured in the explosions. Rescue workers canoed downriver into Karlín. Had Tee and Katka gotten out? Pavel scraped his shoes on the ladder and muttered to himself, "You'll be sorry." Rockefeller pretended not to hear.

In the morning, Rockefeller would walk back to Pavel's house to fetch them breakfast, and entering through the kitchen door, would hear voices. In the morning, after painting water all night, Pavel would outline a body in the bottom corner of a flood. Rockefeller would return to the café unsure how to bring up Tee and Katka, but in the mural, he would recognize the tint of the drowned body, the wave of black hair. And Pavel would step down from the ladder and rest his casts on a rung. "You promised. I need you to stop Tee. Blind him, drown him, just make sure he leaves." Rockefeller would wish he felt more surprised.

CHAPTER 4
THE HUNDRED-YEAR
FLOOD: TEE AND
KATKA

I

The day before the flood, August 12, 2002, the rain fell from early in the morning, but Katka didn't show. Tee went to an Internet café to escape the wanting. At the top of his in-box was his mother's e-mail. He read it in a daze. When he left the Internet café, he forgot his umbrella, but he didn't think this linked him to Katka. He kept moving. Strangers shuttled by in the rain. Back in his apartment, he took down the painting of the Russian tank treading over a woman—over Katka—in Old Town, his final thank-you for modeling. He had meant to do so ever since his trip back to Boston. He hung Mucha's "Seasons" instead: four half-nude women for a year. From his dresser, he removed the last stolen objects and set them in clear view. He wasn't hiding. Outside, the streets echoed, and he cursed the constant construction. He swept and mopped and washed dishes and waited for another man's wife. Once, he almost called the Globe to ask where Ynez had gone, single Ynez. She had quit, at least in part, because of him. How should he understand that? He held his phone like one of the objects on his dresser, like it didn't belong to him except by whatever mysterious instinct had made him take it. What if Ynez had gotten pregnant? What if Katka got pregnant? Would that unite or split them apart? What was his birth mother like pregnant? The tremor of skin as he kicked inside? By the time Katka appeared on the sidewalk below, in the night, her head bent and water slicking off her dark brown hair, he was dialing his father.

He hung up and pressed the buzzer to let Katka in. He timed his steps to the door with her steps on the stairs. Then he pulled her inside. He kissed her rain-wet lips and hugged her as she shivered. What had happened in Korea twenty-two years ago didn't matter like the woman in his arms now. He slipped his hand up under the wet back of her blouse. Her cool skin, her cold lips, grew warm. He kissed her neck, swept her hair over her ear, and when a knock came at the door, he answered it as if there were two of her.

Rockefeller stood before them. For a moment Tee thought he was dreaming. He'd exposed Katka—he could read this in Rockefeller's trembling chin, though Rockefeller had said he knew about them. The difference between knowing and seeing. Katka shivered in her wet clothes and covered her chest.

A flood? Tee felt flooded by memories that could confirm or disprove his mother's e-mail. "What are you talking about?" he asked. Rockefeller whispered in Czech, and Katka slipped into the bedroom. Briefly Rockefeller's face reddened. He backed out.

"Rockefeller," Katka said, when she returned to the hall. She rubbed her lips, and Tee kissed her bitterly. When their mouths parted, she said, "I was not trying to make you to kiss me."

He held his breath and kissed her again. "I'm sorry," he said. "Rockefeller already knew about us." He remembered the bustle, earlier, outside his window.

"I have left Pavel," she said.

Immediately Tee was in Korea. His father stood over him, deciding. Tee's container filled. He tugged at Katka's wet blouse. The fabric bunched and stuck to her skin, as he rolled it upward, awkwardly. It covered her eyes, and he kissed her while she was still blind. She shivered and slipped free of the blouse, turned for him to get her bra.

He licked one nipple, then the other. Her breaths grew louder. She peeled off her underwear and he led her toward the bedroom. They made it as far as the couch—she still had on her boots, he still had on his shirt and socks. She bit his shoulder as he moved inside of her, and he said, "You have left him."

"You heard that, then. My marriage is over."

He pressed her against the arm of the couch. He felt her hip bones, hard sharp curves under his fingers. She was his birth mother, he admitted in that instant. He was his father. Her long black hair, three freckles beside her mouth. He didn't even have to transform—in his mind's eye, he had always been a white kid with a curved nose and raised eyebrow.

He kissed her collarbone. She moaned. He fit his hips into hers, pulling her waist with both hands. He wanted to be deeper. He pushed against her. He wanted to be so deep they might switch bodies: he white, she Asian. He shut his eyes, and she pulled him onto the cushions. He slipped an arm around her, under her armpits. Her back was strong and athletic. She raked her nails down his ribs. He moved faster, panting now. She arched her chest into his, he felt their sweat and heat. Her skin slick already. She was turning her hips slightly, in rhythm. His eyes were still shut. He wondered if she had noticed he wasn't looking at her. But then she called his name—and he heard her voice, he kissed her mouth, he felt her breasts. She held him still for a moment, and he opened his eyes. She rocked her hips again, cradling her arms around his back, and he returned to his senses.

II

As soon as Katka had stepped away from the house in Malešice, just after midnight, she had heard the signs of the flood for the first time. All day she and Pavel had moved from one room to another, not eating, yelling at each other to stop, please, and listen. Around sunset the phone interrupted them, twice, and then a third time, and he kicked the cord free of the wall. She insulted his art, then she forced herself not to apologize, then she pitied him. They argued in the kitchen, alarmingly close to the knives.

When she said at last that she was cheating, he paled and said, "You're lying? The American?" She could hardly believe it when he mumbled that she was a gypsy whore like her grandmother. His casts crashed the dishes on the counter to the floor, and she grabbed her calf. Her leg pulsed. Her fingers came away red. She reached past him for a kitchen towel, held her breath, and pressed the towel to the cut. He reached forward, as if to help. She heard his casts scratch together, his latest tic, and he stepped back again. She pictured Tee's wide forehead, which already wrinkled when he grew skeptical. Once, sweeping up after a meal, she'd told Tee to keep his feet on the floor or he would never marry, and his forehead had creased so deeply he didn't look like himself.

"He doesn't even know who he is," Pavel said.

Later, after she left him, she walked alone under the streetlamps to the stop for the 51 night tram. The light shone close to the posts in the rain. She had forgotten an umbrella. The rain beat down, wetting her hair to her head. A couple stumbled along drunk, talking about the flood. A siren rang out in the distance. She would catch the 51 and then the 52, and hopefully, Tee would be awake when she surprised him. He would be in the same private space as she, ignorant of natural disasters, his Czech poor and his flat without telly or radio.

Her heel caught an edge of the cobblestone, and the pain in her calf squirmed up her leg and into the roots of her teeth. Rainwater slid down the side of her boot and stung her. She walked slowly, watched where she placed her feet.

She tried not to feel alone.

The tram came after five minutes, pulling up without its lights on—malfunction, she wondered, or error. She recalled an accident weeks earlier. A tourist had crossed the tracks without looking, and the tram flipped over trying to avoid him. She sat by the door and held the safety bar over the seat in front of her. Her hands still trembling from leaving her husband. Water dripped off her hair into her lap.

She imagined Tee, asleep in his apartment in the middle of Karlín. Soon she would be beside him—at night, for once—his warmth against her cold skin. She saw his smooth shut eyelids, under that wide forehead, as he slept. She didn't worry yet about the flood. Though legend had it that Old Town would be destroyed by water, the believer in her was all burned up.

As the tram neared the city center, wooden blockades appeared, many with white sandbags piled in front of them, especially closer to the river. They pulled into Karlovo Náměstí. In the square, she noticed people arguing, a tension in the night, fewer cars than usual.

She stepped down to change trams. Nearby, two skateboarders argued with a policeman. They said their families wouldn't leave home for a flood that would never come. The policeman said he was only passing through. He said evacuation orders were, as far as he knew, rumor. She saw more sandbags, piled up like the city was in a war.

A woman walked up to her and asked if she had a light while her brother or boyfriend or husband held a golf umbrella over the three of them. Katka shook her head, but asked about the weather. The umbrella kept the water out of her boots.

"Oh, you poor dear," the woman said, noticing her lack. "Keep it over her." She touched the arm of the man, probably her lover. He held the umbrella higher so Katka didn't have to hunch.

The man said hadn't she heard? The rain was supposed to fall all day again tomorrow, and maybe the day after as well. He said the Vltava would rise up into Old Town and throughout the Jewish Quarter to Karlín.

Katka shivered and thanked them for the shelter.

"We're here on vacation from Plzeň," the woman said. "What bad timing!"

The man smiled and kissed her forehead. Katka stayed under the umbrella until the 52 came. As the couple walked away, the woman said there were still kind strangers out there, as if Katka had said there weren't.

The tram went through Wenceslas Square, where a number of drunk youths crowded on, and she thought about her husband, rubbing his casts together in the rain. It was a simple decision, she thought. She felt the press of Tee's hands on her waist. Tee had climbed the tree after her; Pavel had tried to knock them down. The best Pavel could manage anymore was a painting of Tee.

A man on the tram leaned in and asked if she was okay, and she wiped her eyes and said, "And what would you do if I am not?" He turned away.

She got off the tram in Karlín and walked along the street toward Tee's flat. She remembered him coming to the hospital to check on Pavel's wrists—she'd tried to love only her husband, but as she walked away, she carried Tee with her, like a word on the tip of her tongue.

Later, in his apartment, when they lay on the floor beside each other, cooling off and turning transparent, like a glass slid out of a kiln, he turned on his side and went quiet. He pulled off his shirt, rolled his socks off his feet. He needed to say something but couldn't. Through the doorway to the bedroom, she caught the shape of Pavel's Golem on his chest of drawers—the same statue? She ignored the pain in her leg that returned as the endorphins from making love faded. She waited, and knew they should leave, but decided not to say so until he talked himself out. Tiredness soaked through her, as wet and heavy as the rain. All day she'd been leaving: one place for another, one lover for another, one generation for another. She wanted to stay, she didn't want to go anywhere that held even the threat of her husband, but she also knew they had to get out of Karlín.

III

He touched the five chicken-pox scars on his chest. Then he spread her fingers out with his own until their two hands formed five little steeples, like in a children's rhyme he couldn't quite recall. He moved her fingers over the scars and she stretched her fingertips to align with the dots. "What is wrong?" she asked.

When her hand moved, he told her about his birth mother's photograph, how he'd caught the two diseases in the woods, trying to share as much as he could. He said when he was fifteen, he'd found his mother alone in his room—his adoptive mother—staring at the photo. "I discovered it under your socks?" she said. "You have her eyes, at least?" She seemed about to add something more, to explain that lingering "at least," but his father's car hummed in the drive. She dropped the photo and sucked her lips between her teeth. He felt his container filling. After she left, he threw the photo away in the bathroom, so she wouldn't find it in his bedroom again. He thought she was angry with him, or heartbroken. He worried that she might think he cared more about his birth mother than about her. But he was also ashamed to be caught, ashamed that he'd been looking at the photograph night after night. Later he dug it out of the trash can and hid it in a wallet he never used.

He told Katka he'd made his birth mother, in his mind, into a woman who wished to leave Korea; he'd made lives for her in which she met foreigners and fell in love. He said, "I wanted my birth to be planned, I guess. I wanted to be born out of love. Even if that meant my birth father had broken her heart by the time I was born."

He held Katka's hand over his chest again. "Now I know I had nothing to do with love. I found out today—yesterday. My mom sent me an e-mail. She didn't even call. My dad never adopted me. He slept with my birth mother."

He rubbed his face on his shoulder. "How could I not have known?" he asked. "We look similar. Mom said I used to ask about my adoption when I was a kid, and later, I just stopped."

Katka swerved her boots across the floor, and grimaced. "Go on," she said when he paused. He shook his head.

"I don't have anything else to say," he said. "Dad used to say the instant he saw me, he knew we were family. He used to say that all the time. I thought his love was a choice."

She said, as if reading his mind, "Your life is your own."

"Yes," he said. "But only if you admit what you're doing. I went to the same college as him, I left my mom behind, I got into an affair. I didn't even realize, until now, that I was replaying my past."

"You have not got into an affair," she said, her eyes red. "I have done. And it is not an affair. I left him."

"Maybe you're right," he said. "It's not the same." But the words died in his mouth.

"You are an asshole if you think you are just replaying something with me."

A feather caught in his throat. The rain echoed around them, drumming on as the sun rose. He lay with his back flat on the floor, and after a while, she rested her head in the crook of his arm. The hardwood was cool as he smoothed his hand over it, but there was nothing to hold or stow or take.

IV

She listened to him talk about affairs as she pictured the progress of the flood, how high and how far into Karlín, and where they and her husband and Rockefeller were in it. It would have been easier for his father to abandon him, but she didn't say this. He shifted over and knelt above her. He felt the same desire she'd felt, to lose himself in making love. He kissed her and slid his hands under her. Her skin tightened. She would forget, eventually, the times Pavel had lifted her in his arms—on their wedding night; out of the Bay of Angels, on their honeymoon in France; up from the dust, her fingers around his casts. Tee laid her down on the bed and tried to take off her boots, but she brought his hands to her chest.

When they finished, it was day. The sun shone through the window and her hips ached pleasantly. She tried to think about the flood, but she couldn't concentrate. He slept with such whimpering relief that she couldn't keep her eyes open, either. She knew she should wake him and say they must leave, but she longed for sleep. She longed to sleep beside him.

V

He pretended to sleep until she slept, and then he slept lightly enough to hear the knock on the door. He dressed and went to answer it, not wanting to wake her and still in his dream. He'd been running through his parents' house and had fallen between the slats of hardwood into a strange land he knew was Korea but which looked like the half-formed set of a movie, full of uncompleted machines.

At the door, a policeman spoke firmly in Czech. Tee wondered if he was being arrested, before he remembered the flood. A train rumbled in his mind. He felt in his pocket for his cell and saw the message from Rockefeller: *Send her to husband.* Tee remembered being brought home by an officer, once, when he was seven, for shoplifting. His father had said, "He's not my kid. Better take him to jail," and Tee had felt lost and drifting, as if he really was at the wrong house, instead of how he should have felt: *confined,* like a prisoner.

He heard a sound in the hall behind the policeman, but nothing was there. He hadn't seen the ghost once since—when? Since he knew Katka was his alone? If the water did rise and cut them off from the rest of Prague, they would be unreachable, even from text messages, even from e-mail, even from their pasts.

"*Nerozumím*," Tee said, waving his hand. "*Nerozumím*." What did he look like to the policeman? A half-white foreigner who couldn't be bothered to learn Czech. Tee kept the door closed enough so the policeman couldn't get a foot inside.

The man lowered his hands to the floor, saying, "Vltava, Vltava," and lifted them, faster and faster, up his body. He pointed to Tee. "You." He drew the level of his hands up over Tee's head and blew out his cheeks as if to hold his breath before he drowned.

"*Nerozumím*," Tee said again, though he understood.

The policeman jabbed his finger down the stairwell and Tee heard the word for *water*. The man took out a cell phone. "*Moment*," he said, dialing. Tee tried to think of a way to get him to leave. Then a voice said, "Hello? Hello?" The man held the phone through the crack of the door. When Tee took it, a voice said in broken English that it was the police. The flood had gotten into the first-floor apartments and he must pack a single suitcase and evacuate to government housing at one of the selected universities.

Tee pushed the phone back through the crack. The danger of the flood was nothing compared to the danger of someplace Pavel could reach them. As he searched for a way to avoid evacuating, he realized he hadn't said anything yet in English. Before he could change his mind, he bowed a deep Korean bow. "*Annyeong haseyo*," he said.

Now the policeman was the one who said "*Nerozumím*," faltering.

Tee took the opportunity to throw his weight into the door, afraid of Katka waking but more afraid of Katka waking before the policeman left. He surprised the man, and was able to get it shut. He shifted the dead bolt, locked the handle. He held his breath as he imagined the policeman breaking down the door.

From the other room, Katka whimpered with sleep, and he made himself wait to go to her. Outside came a frustrated huff, and then footsteps.

Still he waited. The morning sun shone brightly. In the end it was clear Tee wasn't worth the trouble.

VI

Later Tee would wish he had pulled off Katka's boots as she slept that day. He watched her chest rise and fall, the curve of her body the same as in Pavel's painting. She had kept her boots on as they made love, and now she slept in them. He wondered if she planned to walk out again so soon. The wet boots should have felt awkward, but they thrilled him. That pornographic trope.

After the flood, he would wish she'd simply shown him the cut. Maybe she didn't because she was afraid he would want to protect, or avenge, her. Or she thought showing him the cut meant letting Pavel into the room with them, her leg as clear a warning as a third eye. Maybe she wanted to avoid Pavel and Rockefeller as badly as he did.

He never understood why she didn't say the one thing that would have made him focus and say, yes, they should leave, of course, his past had to wait.

As he watched her, his breaths matched rhythm with hers, and the rise and fall of her breasts mirrored something within him. Outside, he heard an explosion, but the danger was far off. Even the ghost was gone.

VII

Somehow, somehow, she'd fallen asleep. The flood covered the streets now, rubble washing into Old Town. She sat up and stared across the room at Pavel's Golem. She'd bought it as a joke and he'd kept it as a good luck charm. She looked for his latest painting, but then her leg throbbed and she remembered where she was. Rain tapped at the window. Tee sprawled across the sheets, snoring lightly, a cute, predictable snore. Her toes were wet. It was the first time in a dozen years that she hadn't slept beside Pavel. Where had Tee got the Golem?

She stepped slowly toward the bathroom. Out the window, Prague was a layer of water. Inside, the room was as small as her leg. Her calf stung. She wriggled her toes, and she wanted to get rid of the remaining rainwater from the walk over. She felt dirty, a part of the flood. On the couch, Tee's phone rang. She picked up quickly, not wanting to wake him, and it was his father.

"Are you my son's girlfriend?" his father said, his tone patronizing. She realized he must think she was a twenty-two-year-old girl. "Put him on."

"Do you think you have got the right to ask me that?"

"Excuse me? Tee called me earlier."

"You need to be a better father to him," she said, and hung up. From the whine in his voice when he said Tee had called him earlier, she knew that his father would not call again. She felt sorry for Tee, but no matter what he said about accepting the past, she wanted him to think about her when he looked at her. America was too much on his mind. Maybe that was what Pavel had meant about Tee holding the door for himself, not even long enough to let himself through. Or maybe it was just about how Tee looked Korean but was American.

She turned the phone to vibrate. Tee had two messages. One was from a woman, Ynez. The other was from Pavel: *You be sorry.* In the bathroom, Katka ran the faucet over a facecloth, then wiped down her body. She was naked except for the boots.

The name Ynez was familiar, but she couldn't think why. She sat on the edge of the tub and pictured a girl in a hotel. She wondered what Pavel had meant by *You be sorry*—you will be sorry, or you are sorry? It seemed a crucial difference. She eased off the boots, the right first, over her uninjured leg. When her right foot came out dry, her mind emptied of any other question. Not water inside. She didn't want to see what was there, yet she wanted it away from her. She got the left boot off in the tub and a palmful of blood spilled out. The blood stained the porcelain red. She didn't want to look, but she wiped the tub clean with the facecloth and rinsed the cloth in the sink. She opened the medicine cabinet. Empty. How young and unprepared Tee was. She wrapped some toilet paper around her calf and slipped the boot back on.

The leather rubbed the wound, and she bit down the pain. She hobbled back to the bedroom. Outside, a family at the end of the street stepped into a plastic raft, father lifting daughter. It was late afternoon now; the sky was already dark. She and Tee had slept through the entire day as the river rose toward them—she should never have fallen asleep. She should have convinced him to leave immediately. They should have gone to a hotel near the Castle, on high ground.

She shook Tee awake. "*Potopa*," she said, gathering her clothes. She dressed, not wanting him to see her in only her boots, wanting to get out quickly. She would deal with the cut later. "*Potopa*."

"What?" he asked. "Where are you going?" His voice strained.

She slipped her blouse over her head.

"Please," he said. "Come back to bed."

"We must leave." She pointed out the window, at the water instead of the street. The family pushed down into Old Town in their raft. "We cannot get stuck here."

"You're panicking," he said. He got off the bed and picked up her jean skirt. He held it away from her.

Then she realized. "You want to get stuck."

He tossed the skirt on the bed and put his arms around her. She wanted badly for those arms to make her forget the rest of the city— but she refused to regret that forgetting later. She pushed him away.

"It's true," he said, his black eyes shining. "I want to be stuck here."

She darted forward, twisting her leg. She got hold of the skirt and pulled it on, then rested her hand on her chest, breathing deeply. She brushed off her skin as if a bug had landed on her.

"Would it be so bad?" Tee said, frowning. "Just to stay here with me? Until the flood has passed?"

She turned and walked into the hall. "I am afraid of drowning," she said, not wanting to fight. He followed.

"There's no way you're going to drown. We're on the second floor." He grabbed her wrist. "Please."

"How can you be so sure it will never reach us?"

He leaned in, and kissed her neck, and she tried not to feel angry, like she'd only fallen asleep because of him. She reached for the chicken-pox scars on his chest, but then she dropped her hand to her side.

"The water's not that high," he said.

She opened the door, blinking, and stepped down the first few stairs. If it was not that high, they could still walk out. The throbbing was bearable.

"Stop," he said. Below, the light in the hall reflected back at her.

He stomped down behind her and she imagined the splashes he would kick up as they left. Her eyes adjusted to the dark stairwell. Then she saw what made the reflection. Water. Already up to her knees, at least. Almost to her waist.

No, she thought. She kept descending.

"Whenever my dad left the house," Tee said, "someone got hurt."

She lowered her boot into the flood, testing its depth. But after weeks of climbing up to his door, she knew these stairs. His footsteps stopped just behind her. The water rose to her ankle, her shin, a couple centimeters from the lip of her boot, and he coughed behind her until he was choking. Like longing had caught in his throat. Or he had realized at last that they were not safe.

If she wanted out now, he would have to carry her. She knew enough not to let the water in her cut.

"Let's go up to the roof," he said. He stepped into the water, barefoot, and put a hand on her shoulder. "The flood will never reach us."

"You promise," she said.

"I promise."

If it was between protection or rescue, she would rather be protected. She was tired of running into danger, climbing up trees with no way down. "Okay," she said. "The roof."

He turned and went up. Of course the roof would never flood. She couldn't let him carry her. She took the steps gingerly. Tee's black hair dissolved into the stairwell shadows. He was in boxers, as if stepping out to swim. She allowed herself a little hope. He could do that for her. When she was with him, even the history films she liked seemed still undecided.

"Slow down," she said. Then she thought of something else. "Can we even get up there?"

"I am going slow," he said.

On the roof they would only get a little wet from the rain. They'd forgotten an umbrella again.

"If worse comes to worst," he said. "I can swim for both of us."

"You will keep me safe?"

At the top, he tried the door while she waited below, her hand on the stairs and her leg raised slightly, trying not to gasp. For a moment the knob seemed to move in his hand, a trick of the light. Then he put his shoulder into it. Twice. It wouldn't give.

VIII

At sunset they tried to turn on the lights, but the power had failed. He took down birthday candles from a kitchen cabinet, set them in shot glasses on the dining table, and lit one. He rubbed another over the tablecloth, a wax outline: a woman with a baby in her arms. He had never felt his birth mother hold him. The candlelight flickered on Katka's face. She pointed outside and said, "My mum used to say the sunset was as red as a broken heart. She used to say each time you were very sad, you got a freckle."

He had been thinking, he said. Maybe his mother had told him now, after so long, because she had to—something was forcing her hand. Maybe his father had said he would tell, or his aunt had threatened.

"We promised we would not pretend," Katka said.

"What if she's not such a fucking Sherlock Holmes, though?" he said. "What if she's wrong?" But no, he was still pretending. "My dad always said he didn't know my birth mom, that meeting her in the hospital was a coincidence."

He lit another candle and it burned out as he talked. In the shadows, he thought he might see the ghost. Outside, the water rose. His hand sweated in Katka's.

When the sun had set completely, they had nine more candles left from Rockefeller's thirty-sixth birthday in March. They drank warm Krušovice. The refrigerator had sputtered its last cool breath when they opened it an hour earlier. They were hungry but didn't eat. Tee imagined Korea, his birth mother in the bed behind his father, the smell of the beach where a hotel was building a spa to his father's designs. The woman in that bed, touching the swell of her stomach, had been kicked out by her parents. She had put everything on the line for her baby, or for its father. Tee went to light another candle, striking a match that flared up in the dark with a sudden blinding light. A siren rang in the distance, and Katka winced and blew out the flame.

"Save them," she said.

He felt for her in the dark. He elbowed over a bottle and the little beer left spilled across the table. When she lit another match, to clean up, they saw in the spill the wax shape he'd rubbed into the cloth.

IX

Near midnight she pulled him into the kitchen with their long-neglected hunger, and as they made sandwiches, he asked about her father. For a long time, she said finally, she didn't know, or at least understand, that her father was hurting her mother.

Once, when she was eight, she had walked home from school with two girls who said they'd seen her father standing around in the square looking at birds. She told them he'd started collecting feathers instead of butterflies, though this was a lie. When she got home, she found her father scrubbing a stain on the bedroom doorframe. He wiped his eyes as she walked up. On the dark wood, the stain looked almost purple.

"Your mum spilled the wine," her father said, scouring the spots with an old toothbrush. "She's in a bit of a mood."

"Can I help?" Katka asked. She was used to helping with chores.

"No, love," he said. "I'll have got it done in a second."

She fetched two towels anyway and wet them with bleach as she'd seen her mother do. Returning, she said, "These will help, Daddy, won't they?"

He stood. "What are you doing?" he said, fingering his whitening sideburns.

"I can help," she said.

"You know you're not to use bleach." His nose wrinkled, and then the meanness was there.

"What is bleach, Daddy?" she asked. She only knew the word in Czech.

"Bleach," he said. "In your hand, you stupid girl. Bleach. Bleach." He pushed her away and began to cough.

"Stay away from here," he called after her. "Just stay away from here. Please."

When she looked back, his head was slumped against the wall.

She ran to find her mother but couldn't, probably upstairs at their neighbor's. Her father hated the woman upstairs, her gentle questioning.

Outside their neighbor's apartment, Katka heard the woman tut-tutting and the clink of metal and her mother's sharp breaths. When Katka knocked, her mother's voice said, "It is him."

There were scuffling feet and the neighbor's voice behind the door. "It's not him—it's Katka. Should I send her away?"

"Yes," her mother said, then: "No, don't."

Her neighbor said, "Poor girl." The door opened, and Katka ran in.

Her mother held a towel to her face. When she spoke, Katka saw a tooth missing, an imperfection in her cold beauty. "What are you doing here?"

"Maminka," Katka said, "I'm hurt."

"Me, too," her mother said. "Can't you see? Me, too."

Their neighbor took her arm. "Are you okay, Kateřina?" the woman asked.

"Maminka," Katka said, "what happened to your face?"

"Your father," their neighbor said.

Her mother said, "Hush." She walked over and pinched Katka's earlobe lightly. "It was an accident. You know he slams the door. I was chasing after him." The edges of the towel were red. "Come here," she said, bending down.

Katka reached up to her mother's chin. "Does it hurt a lot, Maminka?" The towel shifted slightly and she could see a cut running from the bottom of her mother's eye to the middle of her cheek, before her mother covered it up. "Daddy said you spilled your wine. Are you drunk?"

Her mother stiffened. "Let's go," she whispered. She led her out as their neighbor sighed behind them. They descended the stairs until the door closed.

"Were you drunk, Maminka?" Katka asked again.

Her mother walked down ahead of her until they were at eye level. "Do not say things like that to me," she said.

"I'm sorry," Katka said, not meeting her mother's eyes, that shared blue.

"Look at me, Kateřina. Daddy didn't want to tell you he hurt me, right?"

"I'm sorry," Katka said again, and her mother cupped her two cheeks. She locked their gazes.

"Right?"

Later Katka lay in bed with the wooden doll her father had carved from a branch in the spring, holding the doll's face the way her mother had held her, her hands dwarfing its head. She shook the doll and said, "Bleach. Bleach," as if the word were a curse.

People always said she took after her mother: their eyes, their quiet defiance. But in the end, long after her father killed himself, she left her mother and their secrets behind.

X

The candles blinked out one by one. They could do nothing but wait. He took a candle into the kitchen. They made sandwiches. She offered to cook, but in his refrigerator were only fish sticks, spaghetti sauce, hard-boiled eggs, peanut butter, jelly, half a loaf of bread, shredded cheese, leftover French fries, beer, and milk. They drank the beer. "What are you getting me into?" she asked. "How did you expect to last through the flood?"

"This is what I always eat," he said, then flushed.

They drank a bottle of Krušovice each before another candle burned out. He hadn't expected her to talk about her father's violence. His hands darted over the table. In the dark, she said, "Pavel is not outside the door." She mumbled, as if to herself, but he knew she was talking to him.

"If we were out there," he whispered, "we would have nowhere to go but your house or the café. His house."

"We could go to a hotel," she said.

He remembered the college the policeman had mentioned. "You don't believe I could take care of you."

They stood in the kitchen blindly. Then there was a crash outside, followed by a metallic creaking, and they rushed to the window. Barely any moonlight shone through the clouds. Their eyes adjusted slowly—until they could see a lamp pole hunched over in the water, what looked like a metal bench clinging to the bend.

She turned away. He pressed his forehead to the cold glass.

XI

What if—he said in the dark—in the morning, we see a yellow raft float to the wall and we climb down into it? Years from now, the flood is the beginning of our story. We live in the countryside and grow cabbages and cook gulaš and dumplings and visit your mother.

Katka left the kitchen, in the shadows, her gait unsteady, and he worried he'd upset her. Had he mentioned her mother because of his birth mother? When she returned, she had the pewter Golem he'd stolen from her house. Another double legend, a creature that had killed either by nature or because of lost love. Tee trembled, though he had left it out on his dresser. She placed the figure on the counter. "Pavel has one *just like this*. We can use it to tell the future, if your hob still works."

She lit the stove with the candle. The gas worked. She took his hands and said this fortune could replace the one in his palms. She kissed the Golem's fat belly. "It is the wrong metal," she said. "It should be that metal they used to think could turn into gold."

"Lead," he said, still trembling.

She wiped a pot with a towel, placed it on the burner, and rested the Golem inside. He reached for it automatically and she knocked his hand away.

"I took it," he said. "I didn't mean to. It was just there, in my pocket, when I got home. I meant to give it back."

"And now," she said, "you cannot."

When the pewter had melted down, she asked for a bowl of water. He turned the faucet on and it sputtered weakly—the water, like the power, would soon fail. She poured the liquid metal into the bowl. The pewter swirled in the water in beautiful gray patterns. He held the candle and waited for her to tell him what she saw. But she was choking back tears. "An early death or a coma," he said, reminding her what was in his palms. "Deep loves." She weighed his hands as if they carried the heaviness of his fate. She, too, she said, could picture them with a garden, though in a different country, far from Prague, with flowers instead of cabbage.

"I had bad luck from birth," he said. "My birth mom died, and my dad must have felt like he was stuck with me."

She said: "I wanted a baby, and Pavel put everything else before that."

The candle burned out and they spoke in the dark. "Tell me a legend," he said out of nowhere, and he realized they were making stories of each other, or themselves. "Never mind. Don't."

But she told him about St. Jan of Nepomuk, the queen's confidant, who, despite being tortured, died refusing to expose her confession. The king had him thrown off the Charles Bridge. Katka said Jan's tongue was later found washed up on the banks of the Vltava. If you rubbed his statue on the bridge, you were fated to return to Prague.

"What is he the saint of?" Tee asked.

"Of swimmers. His body swam away and became a ghost."

He asked her to draw the statue. He copied her strokes. A ghost, a fortune, fate. He should have been sick of myths.

- - -

When he lit the third-to-last candle, Katka said she had never learned to swim. She avoided standing water. He could see she was ready to reveal something. "I'm listening," he said. She took his hand and said her father had liked baths, and near the end, the baths had grown longer and longer. She said whenever her father bathed, her mother was unhappy. Her mother used to claim unhappiness marked people's skin, and she would show the marks to Katka: freckles, bruises, scars. Her mother would roll up a sleeve, point to a contusion, and say, "This is from Communism" or "This is from you drawing on the mirror with my lipstick," but never "This is from your father."

One day, the same year her mother's face was split open, Katka sneaked into the bathroom to see her father's bruises, wanting to know how unhappy he was. Her mother had a purple bloom on her thigh because Katka had mouthed off at school for the third time that month. Her father had been in the bath for an hour. After her mother went up to their neighbor's, Katka tiptoed to the bathroom. Her father hated to be interrupted. She put her ear to the wood. Hearing nothing, she cracked the door. Her father's towel, his dirty clothes, wet hair he'd pulled from the drain lay on the floor. She nudged the door a little farther until she could get her head around it.

Steam rushed hot on her face and hazed the air. She was afraid of her father, but she couldn't leave. At first she thought her father's unhappiness must be so bad it leaked, like popped blisters. Dark streaks marbled the water. He didn't respond to her voice. She stepped farther inside, and then she screamed. When her mother finally rushed in, Katka was in the tub, holding her father's wet body.

- - -

The candle had gone out again. Tee shivered. Their families' stories twisted around each other. He had the feeling—as he had when she first told him about her father's suicide—that she knew him by heart. That she had known him, all along, better than anyone else ever could.

"Fathers," she said.

And as if in answer, the ground moaned and shook and the sound of collapsing outside shook them. They hurried to the window. Outside, they could see, at first with difficulty and then all too clearly, an empty space across the street. The green building that used to be there was now a pile of rubble sticking up out of the water, half of the far wall still standing, the lowest apartments settling into the flood with a brick groan. He couldn't help but remember the video of the towers collapsing in New York. Pieces of the building washed along in the current. He imagined a tipping-over like dominoes.

He pulled the shade, and as the sound outside quieted, there was a soft snap in the dark, then a few more in quick succession. He reached his hand out for hers, to where she'd been when he pulled the shade, and he felt the broken pieces of the last two candles drop through his fingers to the floor.

"Oh," she said. "I do not know why I did that."

But they both knew.

He stumbled closer to her and her footsteps padded away. They moved across the room, then went silent. Her breath, her smell, her heat remained. He led out with his arms, and without a word, with nothing but his sense of her, he made his way until her shoulder was against his hand, her fingers rippling through his hair, her lips at his chin, closing in on his mouth.

Later in that darkness, after they made love but before they fell asleep, he said, "When I was young, my uncle used to take me up in his plane and fly me out over the countryside. He only ever seemed happy up there. Sometimes with you, I feel like we're that free. Like we will never come back down." He tried not to think about the buildings falling, or her warnings that they should leave, or her husband on the other side of the city.

"Pavel and I were always stuck," she said. "We were never good for each other. We were trapped in his art."

He shivered, hearing what he'd been hoping to hear since he'd kissed her in the underground café, since she'd pushed him into her closet and he'd seen the ghost.

XII

Katka woke with her leg in her mouth. The cut on her calf ached in her gums. She'd hoped sleep would heal her, seal the skin back together. Instead she felt the boot leather stuck to her wound. The blood had congealed. She'd dreamed of leaving Pavel in the house in Malešice. A large dog blocked her path. As it barked, it changed colors: black, red, green, yellow. It jumped at her throat. She dodged, and it flew past her and landed on Pavel. Suddenly she worried for Pavel's life. She turned back, but the dog was licking his face. She felt the licking on her own face; her cheeks, her nose, melted into water.

Beside her, Tee slept peacefully on top of the sheets. She tried her boots on the floor—before she fell asleep, he'd asked about them, raising the eyebrow he said was from his father. But she saw that they turned him on.

She ground her teeth and lowered her right foot first, then carefully stepped onto her left. Sparks shot up to her hip, and she fell. She clutched the boot and lay on the floor, afraid that she'd woken him. It was too late to leave the apartment, and she didn't want their time together to focus on injury. The cut was not why she'd left Pavel.

When she was sure she wouldn't wake Tee, she limped to the bathroom, groggy with a hangover and the stabbing pain, much worse than before. At the bathroom door, her toes felt wet again. At first she panicked that she'd slept too long—but the floor was dry. The wound had reopened. She'd planted her foot, and the toilet paper must have torn away from her skin, ripping apart the blood clot.

She tried the sink. Nothing came out. She needed to wash the wound. She needed aspirin. Yet somehow the flood was the only water. She rechecked the medicine cabinet—still shockingly bare, still nothing to deserve her faith—then opened the shower curtain.

She poured blood from her boot as if a new ritual, to bleed out each day over her husband. She unwrapped the toilet paper. When she pressed a finger to the cut, something shifted under her skin. She clamped her teeth together. She squeezed the raised flesh beside the cut and covered her mouth to muffle the scream. A sliver of ceramic poked out, just barely, a hint of blue. It must have been working its way out as she slept—how deep it must have lodged. She shivered, her chest shuddered as she breathed, but she held her mouth with one hand, and with the other, she pinched the piece between her fingers and worked the ceramic free until it dropped into the tub.

She couldn't wash the wound. Either she left off the boots and listened to Tee wonder aloud her thoughts—why hadn't she told him before, before the flood got so high?—or she put the boot back on and kept her secret. She rewrapped the cut and wiped the boot dry before replacing it.

As she walked back, another building groaned. She caught the end of the collapse in the window: the roof wobbled as if trying to balance itself, like a drunk; then its bottom fell out and the river sucked the structure under. Slowly.

"You saw it," he said, as if he sensed her in the hall.

She walked into the bedroom, trying to relax her jaw. The floodwater surrounded them, like an ocean around an oil rig, dirty and brown and awash with trash. She was dehydrated—in all this water. The rain had stopped. "It is okay," she said, anticipating him.

"I'm sorry. More than I can say."

She turned and went to the kitchen for the last couple beers she remembered were there. In front of the refrigerator, the tile was wet. A puddle spread over the whiteness to the toes of her boots. The flood had gotten into the apartment.

It took her a while before she realized the refrigerator was leaking, defrosted. Like with the blood in her boot.

He was behind her. "Just the fridge." He took her in his arms, as afraid as she was. "The flood must be washing out the foundations."

She nodded.

He swept one arm backward and into the wall. He shook his hand and they stared at the small dent.

"It doesn't mean this building will fall," he said.

She returned to the bedroom, slowly, to hide the pain, and dressed. He stared at her boots, conspicuous until she was fully clothed. Then he dressed, too. He opened and closed his hand. The red flat of his palm.

When their building didn't collapse after an hour, or a half hour, or fifteen minutes, a long short time, she took off her wedding ring, which she hadn't done before, and left it on the chest of drawers where the Golem had sat. She wished she hadn't slept on the same side of the bed as always.

"You said *potopa* before," Tee said. "What does that mean? Flood?"

She sat on the bed and forced a smile. "I have already told you it is okay. I have already said it is not your fault."

"My aunt tried to jump from the roof the day I got to America," he said, arcing one finger like a diver. "I think she must have known about me. My mother—"

Finally she interrupted him. "Stop it!" she said. "That is enough. Do you see your family here?"

He looked at her in shock. She bit a little flake of skin off her lip until it bled. He opened his mouth to speak, and she said, "If you say you are sorry one more time, I will hate you."

They ate sandwiches again for breakfast, and when they took their dishes back to the kitchen, the flood was there, at last. The water had crept over the linoleum, along the molding in the hall, under the apartment door and across the uneven hardwood. The floor was not flat—Tee had only begun to live on his own.

She pulled him into the kitchen, heaped the peanut butter and jelly and remaining bread into his arms, and nudged him back into the hall, ahead of her. In the bedroom, she pushed him onto the bed. His legs strong from walking all over the city. If the water rose above the mattress, they wouldn't have any choice but to swim. She clambered up beside him. She imagined people in the falling buildings, holding their noses until the magic of survival ran out. Her cheeks rusted. "Do you love me?" she asked suddenly, keeping her fingers from her calf. "Because you had better love me."

When the flood was halfway up the bed, another building fell. Tee got down off the mattress and splashed through the water, his bare calves in the brown river in the bedroom. As he danced through the debris, she smiled that he was still the kid in his boxers in Old Town, the fireworks exploding around him, his black hair flashing like flint under the sparks.

He rescued a few floating books and piled them on the bed, water seeping into the mattress. She smelled the sewage without knowing yet what it was. Her leg beat like a second heart. She imagined them in a country that meant nothing to them—Australia, Papua New Guinea—the paintings and pity and need for secrets fading away. He would write books, and she would learn piano, and eventually they would raise a baby, a red-cheeked, black-eyed surprise. The baby would crawl, stumble to her feet, run around speaking Australian English.

Or at least they would adopt a cat, or a dog—not to wish for too much—take it for walks and let it free in their yard. They would give it a Czech name, and never need to say anything else about their old countries.

At least they would get out of this flood.

One of his books fell open in the water, and she saw, in a margin, her name. She'd violated her rule to not pretend, and she wondered if this meant only pretense was left.

By the time she recognized the long low notes accompanying Tee's dance as the shouts of rescue workers, she was confused again. She dreaded the water—either outside or inside. She wanted to wait for unmistakable danger before she risked swimming. Half-tipsy, half-hungover, she balanced on the mattress and looked out the window. City employees canoed through Karlín. She smelled the water, saw the trash and flotsam in the current, and suddenly, she was sure they must stay.

Tee had noticed the canoes, too. "Who is it?" he asked. "The police?"

"No," she said.

"Rescuers."

"What are we going to do?"

"We can't stay here," he said. "Can we?" He ran out of the bedroom as if he'd been waiting for them, and came back with a couple of plastic bags and stuffed some clothes and books and their cell phones into them.

Her face grew hot and then cold, and a minute passed in which she could have changed his mind but she didn't know what to do.

"Let's go?" he said.

He waited, and finally, she said, "Let us go."

He tossed her one of his hoodies, and she pulled it on over her head. His musty scent in the fabric. "We'll have to jump out the window," he said. She knew Prague's past of defenestration, but perhaps he did not.

He wiped his legs with old clothing and got onto the bed. His skin smelled like the dirty river. He pointed out the window. "Five of them."

She didn't know why she felt wrong about leaving. Had she taken on his beliefs in the end, his earlier us-in-here, them-out-there mentality? "They could be anybody." He shook his head.

When she reached for his fly, he said, "You've kept those boots on since you got here," and, for a liberating instant, she thought that he knew. Yes, she could say, what about her bleeding wound? Then he went on: "I guess I understand holding on to one last piece of your past."

"One last piece of my past?" Maybe it was easiest for him to think she wasn't in danger, simply unable to give up her husband completely.

He called out the window, and the rescuers paddled and shouted back.

"What if you were right and the water never gets to the top of the bed?"

"You don't want me to say sorry," he said, "but this is my fault. And now I can get us out." She let go of him. She hated that he was so eager to save her.

He held up the window, waving at the approaching rescuers. "Can you get some more plastic bags?" she asked. He said there wasn't anything of hers in the flat. She sighed and repeated her request.

When he went to the kitchen, she formed her plan. She would tie bags around her legs so the water wouldn't get in. Then they would swim out to the canoes and leave Prague, visit her mother after all, row out through the rivers into the rest of Europe.

He climbed back onto the bed, wiping himself off with the sheets this time. He never expected to use them again. He smelled even more like the flood. She took the bags from him. The rescue workers shouted warnings. They called, "Titanic. Titanic." They had seen that Tee was a foreigner. A hum rose in Tee's throat and she tied the bags over her boots—both calves, to keep up the illusion. He shot her a questioning glance, but she said, "I know what I am doing," which, unbelievably, kept him quiet. She felt again that he must know. Wind blew in, crinkling the bags. Outside, she thought she saw a yellow bird flap out over the water.

"Ready?" he said. She nodded. He glanced again at what she'd done, frowning, but then he kissed his palm and pressed it to the ceiling. "Good-bye, apartment." He stepped onto the window ledge, his right foot turned sideways. He shoved his plastic bags down the front of his jeans and held out his hand for her.

A desperate longing stopped her breath, as if he'd jumped already, leaving her behind.

"Please," he said.

She took his hand and stepped beside him. She should have run away with him as soon as she could. Maybe every act of faith, as they got older, was meant to make up for an earlier lack of faith. In one movement she made herself small enough to fit through the window and she dropped into the water less than a meter below.

She heard him plop into the river beside her. "Stay there," he said, but she stroked out as fast as she could. She felt the water seep in— inevitably—through the tied-up neck of the bag, and she swallowed the river with a pained gasp. The alcohol in her blood did nothing to dull the burning and pulsing inside her boot. She felt tired, unable to keep churning her limbs. Then, at last, he was there. His arm wrapped beneath her breasts, and he pulled her toward the canoe. A rescue worker helped her in.

"Are you okay?" the man asked in Czech.

"Afraid of water," Tee said, gesturing. He bent over the side, fishing out coasters that floated, trapped, between the canoe and the neighboring building.

This, Katka thought, was how she would leave Karlín: in a lie. She hardly recognized where she was. The river had washed in a brown tide, and the area would never completely recover. The buildings would be abandoned, torn down and rebuilt if they didn't collapse, and the residents, at least many of them, would take the insurance money and move.

Tee was still in the river beside the canoe. She reached between them. In his hoodie, she felt like a second Tee. She was one of her kind, the most American she would ever be, the last American left in this hundred-year flood. She was an identity rising to the surface, as she'd seen him on New Year's. The canoe rocked lightly as he climbed in beside her, and the water dripped off his nose. She managed a smile, and then a grope of fear reminded her that water was unsafe, and she passed out.

XIII

Two other canoes pulled even on either side. The rescue workers gestured for Tee to switch vessels. Katka shut her eyes. Tee shook his head. "*Ne.* I'm staying with her."

The men waved insistently. Tee picked a coaster out of the water—somehow, the objects he'd thrown into the streets days earlier had bobbed up in the flood like echoes.

One of rescue workers said, "You must go other canoe. Many things in Vltava. Hardly go around them."

"Please," Tee said. "I am with this woman."

Their canoeist, a young Czech with a hooked nose, said, "No go, no go."

"Too much dangerous," the other man said. He reached between the canoes and took Tee's arm, at first gently.

Tee called Katka's name. She didn't stir. He had the brief fear that the strain or emotion had made her pass out, but as the yank on his arm unbalanced him, he was forced to shift into the second canoe to keep from falling into the water.

"Will she be okay?" he asked his new canoeist.

"What is on her foots?"

"She really loves those boots," Tee said. "Do you think she is okay?"

"Why not she is okay?" the canoeist asked, paddling them through filthy water.

Tee soon saw why he had been asked to move. When a tree tipped over into the water, the canoes barely swerved around it. The extra weight would have made turning more difficult. A group of workers anchored the trunks underwater as they struggled like ships trying to reach the sea. Tee asked his canoeist where they were going.

"Wait," the man said. A wash of clothes caught on the bow. One of the other men picked off the clothes with his paddle.

"We need to go to a hotel."

"We go near Náměstí Republiky," the man said. "We will put you on ground."

Tee looked for Katka: she lay in the same pose.

Farther down the river, half of a roof bobbed up. The red-brown shingles had blended in with the brown water, and now were only a couple of yards away. He scooped the river out with his hands, to help them turn.

"Do not," the canoeist said, spraying Tee's back as he passed the paddle expertly from one side to the other.

Tee continued scooping. The shingles could be scales on the rising back of a sea monster. The outer two canoes split off in slow arcs, and Tee splashed at the water. He pictured the roof flipping over the canoe and sliding over his head like an underwater coffin. Something slapped his back. The paddle.

"Not helping." The man pointed with the paddle and waited for Tee to stop. Tee sat on his hands. He wanted badly to be with Katka. Her head still lay against the lip of the other canoe. Her canoeist didn't seem to care that she wasn't waking.

The roof carried toward them, individual shingles swirling beside it. All Tee could do was wait. Either the canoe would make it past, or he and Katka would be separated.

The roof seemed to speed up, until it was feet away. They would have to jump out, or they would get hit and fill up slowly. Tee had Katka's cell in a plastic bag down his jeans. She would wake somewhere else and he wouldn't know how to find her. The paddle seemed to bite into the water, bite into the water, and then finally the shingles scraped along the side of the canoe, as they made it past.

Tee checked over the side for a puncture. When he turned and gave a thumbs-up, the canoeist rolled his eyes.

A glint of blue from the other vessel. Katka blinked awake.

They paddled down into the edges of the Jewish Quarter, where the man said the damage was not as bad. In Karlín the sewage systems had caused the current, and the smell, but in other areas buildings hadn't collapsed, the flood wasn't so high or so strong. As they turned in the direction of the Powder Gate, a small black shape darted past. Almost like a seal.

The three other canoes turned off after it, and the men shouted.

"Seal," Tee's canoeist said.

The seal swam around outstretched hands and circled one of the canoes, playing. "How did it get here?" Tee asked, though it must have escaped the zoo.

"They need catching it or could die," the canoeist said. "Three others gone, too."

Four seals somewhere in Prague, or swimming to other cities and countries, miles from the ocean they were seeking. Tee wondered about the rooster that used to wake him.

"They killed elephant earlier," the canoeist said. "So not—" He closed his fingers around his throat.

The seal slipped beneath the bow. "But elephants can swim," Tee said. His mother had taught him this.

"That elephant not."

His mother had taught him about animals, like dolphins, whose breaths were not automatic, who had to choose to breathe.

In the distance, another building buckled into the flood, and Tee half-expected an elephant or some other beast to wade toward them. He had the feeling that the building had been theirs, the one they'd left, and they'd barely lived. He pictured his father's wall-drawings, the faint trace of pencil, despite their erasure.

When the two canoes slid up onto the cobblestone of an inclined street in the Jewish Quarter, Katka's face was drained of color. Tee stepped into the water and helped her out of her canoe. She leaned her long body on him as if she'd broken a leg.

"Find a hospital," she said.

The canoeists called good-bye and pushed off. Tee ignored them. "What's wrong? We got out." As if maybe she hadn't realized.

"Please." She pressed against him. He felt her forehead—she was burning hot. She couldn't walk. The plastic bags, still tied around her legs, sloshed with sludge water. How much did he understand then?

He pulled from his jeans the two plastic bags with his clothing and three books and their cell phones, and slung them over his shoulder. He called a taxi service, but the woman who answered said that the streets were closed. She struggled to make herself clear.

"All right," he said. "I got it. How far do we have to go?"

"Yes," she said. "Close."

He didn't know if she meant close by or closed. She hung up. Later he would be surprised she was still working. It reminded him of the rooster in winter.

He helped Katka down Truhlářská toward the Powder Gate and Náměstí Republiky, dread accumulating in him with each step, like stones in the pockets of a diver. Only a few other people were out. A woman in tiny jeans said something in Czech and Katka replied, wincing. Then a man appeared and pulled the woman away. "Help us," Tee pleaded. But it was each couple for itself.

As they moved, Katka seemed to improve. She limped beside him, not needing his arm for a short period, then needing it again. They closed in on the square. They managed a couple of hundred feet.

"What happened?" he asked whenever she leaned harder.

Finally she said, "It was Pavel."

"How? What did he do to you? Your leg? You've been hurt for how long?"

She looped his arm around her waist. "There is a hospital here if it is not closed."

He eased her along the wet cobblestone and tried not to ask questions she clearly did not want to answer. "A little farther," he said. "Did he hurt you to stop you from leaving him?"

The black top of the Powder Gate seemed to tongue the dark clouds. Katka laid her head on his shoulder. He walked as flatly as he could. As they drew nearer, the dome of the art nouveau Municipal House, then the mural under the dome, then the ornamented facade blocked their view of the Powder Gate. Katka grew heavier on his arm.

Finally she groaned and teetered into him, and he caught her. Her eyes had shut. She'd passed out again. He would have to carry her.

He'd kept her inside as the water rose. He'd waited until buildings fell. He was why she was in Karlín in the first place.

Overhead a helicopter flew by, and he feared his thoughts.

He looked for the hospital, but couldn't find it. He sat Katka down and lightly tapped her cheeks. She didn't stir. Where was he supposed to go? He felt his container fill, with the flood, or with tears, or with the rain they'd thought could hide them. He wished to go back to New Year's, empty properly this time. He shook her, and she nearly slipped into the street.

"Tell me where the hospital is!"

He lifted her, lengthwise, across his arms. He couldn't carry her for long. His plastic bags shifted and he readjusted them.

Seven streets fed into Náměstí Republiky. One led to the hospital. He hurried down the first. She was so tall; he should exercise more. People stared, and he said, "Hospital. Hospital." He knew the word in Czech but couldn't remember it. It stayed just out of reach.

One person quickened her step. Another flipped open his cell phone. The police, Tee thought, that man is calling the police. What did Katka and he look like, in their wet clothes with the plastic bags on Katka's feet and hanging on his arms? He should have removed her bags, at least.

He backed away from the man, who shouted and started after them. Tee carried Katka as fast as he could. The man hesitated, but didn't follow.

Tee went around the corner of the Municipal House and eased Katka back onto the ground. He untied the bags. His chest hurt. His head was a fist. He wanted to take off her boots and know for sure, but there was no time. A doctor would have to do it. Burns maybe, blisters cracking up and down her leg. "Wake up," he said. He shook her shoulders. Nothing. He pinched her. Nothing. He emptied the bags of water on her face, instantly regretting it.

She flinched, and her eyelids fluttered against each other, and he said, please, please. Until she had come back.

"Tee."

"Just tell me where the hospital is."

"Hybernská. I can go on my own."

He already had her in his arms again. Another street sign, on another building. Then she slapped his chest and told him to put her down, and for an instant she was so much her commanding self again that he did. "Are you okay?" he asked. The city seemed all a gritty brown and her eyes incredibly blue.

She grimaced and led him around a corner where a sign for Hybernská was hidden. He would never have found it. As they limped toward the hospital, his cell phone vibrated. Probably his mother—she would have heard about the flood. But only Katka mattered.

CHAPTER 5
MEMORIES OF
WATER

I

In Boston, in the hospital and then in the rehabilitation center, Tee's parents visited together every other day, an effort he tried to appreciate. On odd days, they alternated. When they came together, they would drill him on the date. His OT made him write the date at the end of each session, chronicling his confusion. With his mother, Tee talked warily about the future—she made plans, got a new library job, put the house on the market. With his father, Tee played memory games. Often he forgot the rules, moving twice in a row even when his cards didn't match. He would remember Katka's uncharacteristic competitiveness. His father would point to the difference in the cards, as if the mistake was in the pictures.

Tee walked farther and farther on his own. He wanted to look for the ghost woman without being judged when he fell. He kept checking his watch to be certain the hands moved. One morning she seemed to be reading in the rehab library—he saw her silhouette in the picture window. But inside was only the Korean girl who believed she was losing her memory, though she was not. Her memories didn't seem right to her. She tapped the seat beside her, and spoke spell-like English. She wanted to know if Tee was Korean. He didn't know how to answer.

To him, Korea was another abstract noun. He asked about Busan, but she was from Seoul and hated the beach. When she asked why he never learned Korean, he stood and browsed the shelves. He borrowed an anatomy book, and stayed up late that night tracing over tibia, fibula, femur, patella, quadriceps, peroneus, soleus, gastrocnemius. He found the cerebellum and amygdala in the brain, where the staff had claimed they were.

When he looked out the window now, he read the potential for storms. In one of his recurring nightmares, he stood under a clear sky while something—water or blood—dripped on his head. The worst dreams were the ones of the flood, watching Katka jump from the windowsill, unable to save her yet not wanting to wake and lose her twice.

One day he found a puzzle in the media room. With every piece, he would forget what he was making. When he finally finished it, it wasn't what he'd thought it would be.

As he walked around the rehab center, the ghost popped up in unexpected places: going out the emergency exit, passing through the fish tank, getting a drink of water. He wondered why it had disappeared during the flood in Prague. Was that disappearance meant to help or to hurt him? Why was it back now? In his mind, he kept turning over the same stones. Under which was the truth?

He should have cared more about Katka. He thought back to the paintings. What had the artist and the artist's wife really seen in him? A boy propping the door for himself, then letting it shut.

He still didn't know what Pavel had meant by that, yet he could remember it when he forgot so much else.

He walked with his father through the four atriums. "What does it mean if someone says you hold the door for yourself?" he asked.

"You mean just, you open the door?" his father said. He was growing a beard like Tee's uncle's. Did he even realize he was doing this, taking a cue from the dead?

"Just, you open the door?" Tee repeated.

"If you're holding the door for yourself, that means you've opened the door and are about to go through it."

Tee wondered if that was what Pavel had meant, the confusion just English as a second language. But Pavel had said the person behind Tee was Tee himself.

The next time his mother visited alone, it was a Sunday. She was wearing a yellow sundress he recognized but couldn't place. She dragged him to mass in the center's prayer room, where once a week a priest stopped in from a local parish—most likely for the extra collection. Tee knew how meagerly belief paid. He wanted to ask his mother to interpret Prague, but he felt paralyzed by her desire to heal him. She held his hand. The mass was a mass of remembrance. The priest called out names of the dead and tolled two heavy bells. As the bells harmonized, Tee's breaths slowed. Beyond the tolling he sensed the pressure of an expanding silence, as if the bells were ringing in the ocean at high tide. He wished his uncle were there, as if the priest had said "Hi" in greeting, not as one of the names. His uncle would have known what to tell him. Tee had always thought "Hi" was a good name for a pilot. But maybe his uncle would have been a better phone solicitor, or customer service rep, someone who had to keep his feet on the ground and listen. He was a good listener, which he had claimed helped him read the weather. When the tolling faded, Tee followed his mother back to his room. She asked what was on his mind, but he kept hearing the bells, the chanting of names, and then the silence.

||

One night, after his parents had come and gone, Tee lifted the typewriter onto his lap tray and tried to write about Korea. He wondered how his father and his birth mother had communicated. When they went out to dinner, how did people treat him, the foreigner who couldn't even understand the woman he'd impregnated? Was she sad? Happy? His father must have felt far from her then, from the baby and her. Though later, when her ribs hurt and she couldn't breathe, she pulled him in with a closeness he'd never experienced, as if the physicality of their bodies could steady them.

Tee wrote, for a while, about sympathetic pregnancy, which he had learned about from one of the other rehab patients, a woman whose husband had left her after their baby died. He wrote about his father taking on his birth mother's hormones and desires. Would his father have been that kind of man? His father grew rounder, too. He felt hungry and hot and emotional, too. Slowly he saw that this was a symptom of love. He stood at the mirror, rubbing his belly, his body comprehending what he did not. In the hospital they listened to the whir of Tee's heart like the motor of an airplane. The baby was always there, always directing them with a hidden, mysterious force.

Tee wrote that when his birth mother was so big she could barely move, his father brought leftovers from a hotel party. She met him on the stairs, having waited up for the food. He lifted the bag to his nose and sniffed it, teasing her. But then her cheeks flushed and she lost her balance. He saved the food first, thinking of the baby ever ravenous, and almost missed her. She fell on top of him. At first he thought she was going into labor. He had one leg braced where the stairs met the wall, and he felt the snap as her weight landed. In that moment, maybe he sensed what the future held—he would snap everything to save what was inside of her.

Tee didn't know. He let the rhythm of the clacking keys and the answering echo of the letters fill his head. He loved that sound of causation, of the tap tap tap making the words exist. Before he touched the keys, there was nothing but white space. He typed until he needed to stretch, to get the voice of his father out of him, to get out of Korea. He was far from his birth land, a country he knew nothing about. He knew nothing about his father's relationship with his birth mother. He walked down the hall to the nearest window. The trees outside the rehab center, real trees, rustled in the wind. There was going to be a storm. He listened for the sound of rain or river, thinking about the iterations of names, Charles River, Charles Bridge, and the steady flow of water accumulating until it reached an ocean, or a sea, a place where it would be swallowed up by more of itself. In Korea his father had found a thermal spring deep beneath the ground, and turned it into pleasure baths. His father had broken a leg and decided to take Tee home. Had he broken it to save a hidden life, a life he might have changed for, if Tee's birth mother hadn't died? If she hadn't died, where would Tee be now?

CHAPTER 6
THE POSSIBILITY
OF SAINTS

I

Not until after Prague, when Tee was in a hospital himself, in Boston, could he ask the nurses and doctors the questions he'd wanted to know about Katka. "What would you do if a woman came in from a flood with a cut on her leg?" They humored him. They said they would examine the leg, check for a fever, and determine if the wound was infected, which, in a flood, it might be. Then they would put her on antibiotics and send her home.

"How could you tell if it was infected?" Tee asked. A fever, or redness, or swelling, or loss of blood pressure. Or sometimes they said, "Thomas, you need to rest" or "Thomas, I've answered that question a dozen times already. Do you remember?"

He asked what kind of antibiotics they would put her on. A wide spectrum. They would take a culture to find out what she had.

He asked would they really send her home. They would, unless the cut looked very bad and they saw signs of NF or other serious diseases.

He asked what signs they would look for. They asked why he was interested, and he shut up, or occasionally he pressed on. The leg might be twice its size, or beet red and the skin eaten away, or filled with pus.

He asked about NF. Necrotizing fasciitis, flesh-eating bacteria, rarely found. More common was sepsis, bacteria in the blood that could lead to shock.

He asked again about sending the woman home. If someone thought she had one of these diseases, the doctor might keep her overnight. Or sometimes, when Tee asked, they noticed his shifting eyes. Sometimes they grew awkwardly quiet. They would say, probably she would be sent home, especially if the hospital was busy, as in a flood. Or they would politely ignore him, which was easier, and simply do their jobs.

In Náměstí Republiky, the doctor did almost exactly what Tee would be told a doctor should do. The cut was stitched and dressed, Katka shot with antibiotics and prescribed a number of pills which Tee managed to get from the basement pharmacy.

When she took off her boots, her wound showed, at last, red and irritated, giving off a heat of its own. But not nearly as bad as he'd imagined. A nurse took a culture and Katka spoke to the doctor in Czech. They checked her fever, and it wasn't high enough to keep her there, so they sent her home to return if needed.

Tee imagined Pavel pushing Katka over into the glass coffee table, or smashing a window, or throwing something sharp. He didn't ask. They stepped out of the hospital and back into the square, Katka in hospital slippers, and they went through the options. The hospital had mentioned the university shelter.

"We could try it," she said.

He pictured a mass of people disturbing her rest.

"We could check hotels."

But he said what she knew, that the hotels would be booked by earlier evacuees.

"You were right," Tee said. "We should have left before."

She didn't suggest the house in Malešice. She didn't remind him she had a bed of her own. He knew himself where they had to go.

||

When they got there, the house was empty. Where was Pavel with a flood outside? Tee insisted on sleeping on the floor. Without discussing it, they faced the painting of her toward the wall, and she fell asleep instantly, her leg wrapped in gauze under the sheets. He blinked awake every hour or so, afraid that Pavel would return. The doctor had said her leg was infected. Tee had promised her safety.

He woke to her moans. He climbed out of the pit of sleep until he was back in her house. He pinched his neck to get his blood going, and knelt beside her. When he lifted the blanket, heat sighed from the wound. He wondered if he was still dreaming. Her calf was bright red, an apple dangling from her knee. As if he could slip the fruit out from under her skin and tuck it into his pocket. "God," he said. "We have to go back to the hospital."

She said immediately, "My leg." She reached down, and when her fingers brushed the gauze, a cry escaped her. She gasped and cried—both at the same time. He searched the plastic bags for his cell. There were nine missed calls, all his mother. He dialed emergency. He held the phone for Katka, his hand trembling, and he worried that he would hurt her ear. She managed their address and a few details in Czech.

He asked if she needed water, ice. He would get some ice. "I'll be back in ten seconds. Ice will help."

He hurried into the kitchen. Thankfully, the power was still on. As he counted down—ten, nine, eight—he let himself cry. He took a bag of peas from the freezer, and returning, he heard her muffle a moan.

He hovered the peas above her calf. "This is going to hurt," he said. When the bag touched her skin, she wept haltingly, deep wet breaths. Her hand reached for the peas and then stopped. She bit her lip. And he heard a door open.

The ghost, he thought hopefully. But he knew it was not.

She swiped the peas off her leg, gulping air. He waited for Pavel— when Pavel walked in, he thought cruelly, the affair was over. Her husband had kept her safe through a revolution. Her husband had made her art.

"I should have listened to you," Tee whispered. Then the doorway filled with the giant frame of his neighbor. Tee's back twitched, anticipating a blow. Why Rockefeller? Had the artist asked Rockefeller to stop by? Had they made up?

When Tee looked again, the door was empty.

"They are going to cut off my leg," Katka said. "What if they have got to cut it off?" She'd noticed nothing. But he could smell Rockefeller's sweat despite the sour gauze.

"No one's going to cut anything off."

"Tell me it will be all right," she said.

He said: "Remember, stepping in shit is good luck."

She frowned, and he realized it sounded like a joke. "You'll be all right," he said. "We'll be together. The doctors will fix it."

After another fifteen minutes, they heard the ambulance. Tee hoped Rockefeller was far away now. He said he would go out to meet the EMTs, since it would be faster.

The ambulance parked on the curb. Two paramedics got out without the stretcher, and Tee shouted and pumped his fists up and down at his sides. He ran forward and pointed to the van and mimed again. Minutes wasted.

Back in the bedroom, he rocked on the balls of his feet as they asked Katka questions, as they touched her forehead and lifted her onto the padding. They carried her outside. Tee climbed into the ambulance beside her, but one of the paramedics waved him out. "Who—" the man said. Tee squeezed her hand. She said something in Czech to convince them.

He would have said they were married. Only he didn't know how to say it in Czech, and he didn't have a ring. He was his father, chasing a foreign lover into the ER.

Inside the ambulance, the paramedics gave her two shots and unwrapped the gauze. Tee made an effort not to gag. Her wound had split open, as if her calf had ballooned overnight until the skin had reached its limit and popped. Inside, he could see the layers of muscle, covered in a film of pus. At the edges of the hole, the skin had settled back like two rubber flaps.

Katka tried to sit up, but they pressed her flat against the stretcher. "What do you see?" she said. "Tell me what you see." She spoke Czech to the paramedics, and they glared at Tee as they calmed her. The smell stuck to the walls of his lungs. He wanted to stop staring at the raw insides of her leg, but he couldn't.

They arrived at a different hospital than before. The nurses took her away. He tried to follow, panicked that he would have no way of knowing what was happening. She mumbled something, yet they refused him. "It will be fine," she told him. "They will show you in later." Arriving at the hospital had eased her nerves, as he'd thought it would do for him. Instead he imagined parts of her falling out of the crack in her leg: her kneecap, her liver, her heart.

"How will I know if something changes?"

She said any doctor would speak some English. They rolled her away. A nurse blocked the hall, pointing to a waiting room where a dozen bleary-eyed Czechs sat in chairs along the walls, a cluster of TVs hanging down in the middle, as if no one could have his back to anyone else. Tee's feet squeaked on the white tile. He should call Pavel. On the TV, zoo workers rescued condors drowning in a giant cage. Tee didn't know if the footage was current. It was the third day of the flood. President Havel spoke into the cameras.

When Tee checked his cell for the time—nearly ten—he saw again the nine missed calls from his mother; then, beneath them, the one received call from his father. He didn't remember that call. Had he rolled over in his sleep and hit a button before returning to his dreams? He could call back now, but it didn't matter. Katka was in a room somewhere on the other side of the wall. He pictured a machine that could return her leg to its normal state, as if vacuuming the air from a zeppelin. In a hospital like this, his father had lied to him, his birth mother had asked a foreign stranger to take her baby to America. His entire life, Tee had believed hospitals to be places of love at first glance. New starts.

Katka had tried to give them a new start, and he had asked her to jump into a river of disease. Pavel hadn't hurt her so badly. Before the flood the wound could have been stitched up and forgotten. Tee felt something in his back pocket—a coaster—and he plucked at it until the scraps looked like feathers of some dead bird. On the TV, wooden beams piled up like pick-up sticks in the water. Workers in a motorboat removed the rubble, wearing yellow waders as if to fish. One smiled into the camera; for a second he thought it was Ynez. A chart seemed to show the water receding. Maybe the flood would never have risen as high as the bed. Katka and he could still be making love, she in her protective boots. Though the buildings would still be falling.

As he rewound those hours in his head, a doctor appeared and spoke rapid Czech. Everyone turned at once. Tee heard his name.

He pointed to himself. "*Americky*," he said, not sure he had the right word. "Do you speak English?"

The doctor muttered under his breath and said, "Little bit. You not look American. You are her husband?"

She'd had the same idea then.

The doctor shook his head. "You are too young," he said. "She needs debridement. We take away bad tissue."

Tee didn't care what the doctor said about him—bad tissue they could surely remove.

"Bacteria eats her leg," the doctor was saying.

"Eats?"

The man pursed his lips as if the English had soured. His face was stubbled and haggard; he probably had many other patients. He said her organs were losing a fight against the disease. They had put her on an IV, but now they had to cut away the sick parts of her leg.

Tee asked if he could see her.

"After. Maybe at night."

He was about to ask if she would lose her leg when the doctor turned and left.

As Tee waited, more anxiously now, people came in with coughs and flood-dirty clothes and minor skin wounds. About an hour later, a nurse gestured for him to follow. He hopped up, thinking the doctor would have come if the news was bad. In the hall, the nurse asked, "Do you need for me helping you call her family?"

"What happened?"

The nurse shook her head. "I mean for if you have trouble talking them. I help."

He understood. She was wondering why he hadn't called anyone about the surgery. "I'll call," he said. "It's okay. My wife's family speaks English." Yet he had no phone number for Katka's mother, and the only other person was Pavel.

The nurse nodded and offered her assistance if needed.

At least, he thought as he turned back inside the waiting room, no one had recognized Katka from the paintings. They were too abstract. More real than life. He pretended to dial and raised the phone to his ear. "I have some awful news. Katka's in the hospital. Hurry. Come right away." In the doorway, the nurse smiled.

Tee wondered if there was anyone Katka did want to see. She was getting surgery. No one should be worried unnecessarily.

As the hours passed, Tee couldn't stop thinking. He'd spent all his idle time in Prague so far drawing and taking things, a child carving his name on a tree. He hadn't protected Katka, or himself. He had been more interested in the stories they told each other. He wanted to believe that at any minute she would wake and he would go to her. But then there was her leg, white pus squirming from her flesh like grubs.

The scent of disinfectant, and the sterile walls, and the absence of color, seemed to hypnotize him. After a while he found himself thinking about his non-adoption again, hating that his concentration wavered. He forced his thoughts back to Katka. But the longer the wait, the more his mind wanted to go elsewhere. He wondered how his mother had felt when she first figured out the truth about him. How had she kept it to herself for so long? What more did she and his father know? Did his father know his birth mother's hobbies? her allergies? her extended family? All those questions he'd never thought could be answered. He wondered if his father blamed him for his birth mother's death. Was that why his father had kept her from him?

Tee pictured his mother back in Boston, her familiar frown, patterned with freckles. In one of the oldest home videos, his father's finger traces the constellations on her cheeks, one side and then the other. Once, they were drawn to each other's differences. Before they found out they couldn't have a baby.

It was Tee's fault if he knew nothing about his birth mother. He had tucked his adoption into his pockets, another souvenir.

What he really wanted, of course, was to hear Katka say everything would be fine. He remembered she had wanted him to give her the same reassurances. Was that belief in their belief in each other love?

When his mother called, in the early afternoon, first thing in the morning for her, he answered the phone. Her tenth call.

"I'm here, Mom."

"Tee! Oh, thank God you're okay."

"You almost killed me with that e-mail," he said, unable to resist. He pictured her making coffee, cooking breakfast, the phone cradled against her pale neck.

"I heard there was a flood," she said.

"I'm not okay, by the way."

"What's wrong?" she asked. "What happened?"

"What were you thinking, Mom? Why did you e-mail me that?"

She asked whether he was hurt. "We can talk about the e-mail later. Is everything all right now?"

He said later he would still be angry. He heard her teeth click together. He wanted something motherly from her, a reassurance that she really had sent the e-mail for his good.

"You're not physically injured?" she said. "Your body is still intact?"

"My body is still intact. Why didn't you tell me about her earlier?"

His mother said she didn't have any facts. He heard oil sizzling. She was flipping an egg, or a pancake, her veined fingers tightening around the spatula. "I mean, I know," she said, "but I have no proof. Your father would never talk about it. You must know, too."

His phone slipped in his wet palm. He wished to reach through the line and shake her. He plugged his other ear to hear her better. She walked away from the oil, and her nose whined. "Mom," he said, finally relenting, "I'm in some other trouble here. With a girl."

"You got her pregnant," his mother whispered, as if she, too, thought he had turned into his father.

"I'm trying to talk to you." Before he could change his mind, he told his mother about the infection and the surgery and the swollen leg so big it was like a planet had split a fault. He said he didn't know what to do.

"Where are you?" his mother asked.

"In the hospital."

She asked again if he was okay, and he took his finger out of his ear. "You're not listening. What's debridement? Tell me something I need to know."

"I'm not a doctor."

She was right. He needed to talk to a doctor. His mother just wanted to know that he was okay.

"I didn't get anyone pregnant," he said. "But I am in love with a woman who is older than me, who is from another country. Whatever happened with Dad, those are my feelings. What's wrong with that?"

His mother was silent.

"I'm okay," he said. "Thank you for calling me." He hung up.

He left the waiting room. He had to ignore the language barrier, stop being timid and ashamed. He had to act more American. At the desk, he asked for Katka's doctor. The nurse replied in Czech, but Tee persisted: "Her doctor. Or tell me her room number. I need to see her."

Another nurse came and spoke softly with the first, as if Tee was only pretending not to understand. He asked again whenever they paused. At last they made a call, and Katka's doctor reappeared.

"We are busy," the doctor said. "I have no time."

"If you're here, the surgery must be over," Tee said.

The doctor said something in Czech, and the nurses averted their eyes. "She rests now," he told Tee. "Her debridement is—later you see. We need more time with her."

"I want to see her now," Tee said.

"No. In this, no agreement."

Tee stepped forward; a cold breeze rose from somewhere. Then he said, "She's okay? She'll be okay? There's nothing to worry about?"

The doctor picked at his stethoscope.

"Tonight—let me see her tonight."

"You will see her tonight," the doctor said, and left.

Tee leaned his elbows on the polished counter. Why had his resolve weakened? The nurse behind the desk touched his arm. She gestured for him to move. Heat flashed back up his body into his neck and face, but not like anger, more like embarrassment. He dropped his arms at his sides. The nurse smiled, understanding or pitying him.

"Okay?" the second nurse asked, her glare, too, disappearing.

Tee brushed his hot cheek. They seemed to wait for him to say something. He turned back toward the waiting room. The nurse who'd offered her help earlier hurried up the corridor, but he shook his head, wishing to be alone.

"Nobody is coming?"

"Which room is she in?" he said. "I need to see my wife."

"She not your wife," the nurse said with an accusing smile. "I am checking her papers." He knew what had happened. Meaning to help, she had found Katka's emergency contact. "You are not her *miláček*," the nurse said. "I know that name of her *miláček*."

"I'm her husband," Tee said.

"That painter will here soon," she said. "Who are you?"

He needed her to hear him out—he needed someone to give way. He stepped forward, trying again to assert himself, and she shrank back in sudden fear.

"You know nothing about me," Tee said quietly. "Where do you get the right to say who I am?"

The nurse couldn't make him go since Katka wanted him to stay. Maybe the staff anticipated a good fight. Everyone's eyes seemed to follow him as if they'd bet for or against him. In the waiting room, he took a pen from the side table and weighed his options: he wasn't leaving, and he wasn't letting Pavel take her back. He could only acknowledge that he had hurt her, and hurt Pavel, and yet press on. Later, after Katka healed, they would flee together.

The television showed a barge sinking before it could hit a bridge, and policemen cheering. A plane crashed in Tee's mind.

Sunset was only a few hours off. Tee watched the shadows outside—doctors smoking with their patients—like the creeping fingers of the flood. He remembered how Katka had snapped the last candles, as he pressed the tip of the pen against the table, bending the barrel.

Finally Pavel arrived—with Rockefeller. The smaller and the larger man talked at the desk, presumably about Katka's health. What was their deal? Forgive and forget? Rockefeller stood to the side of the artist and after a while, went out to smoke, ignoring Tee. When Pavel scraped his casts across the counter, no one stopped him. They knew who he was. Either they recognized him or the nurse had told them.

They would tell Pavel exactly what Katka's status was. A nurse pointed toward the waiting room and Pavel tensed and looked over his shoulder. Tee tried to keep his face blank. A corner of his stomach clenched, a muscle he hadn't known he had.

As Pavel entered the waiting room, it went quiet. Heads turned, not to the artist, but to Tee. One of the nurses crossed his arms. Tee plucked at the lip of his jeans pocket, but did not lower his eyes. He imagined how he must look, still in his flood-stained clothes. He'd been exhausted the night before, and in the morning, they'd rushed to the hospital before he could shower. He probably still smelled like the river.

"You hurt her," he said.

Pavel reddened. "She walking out okay. No flood, no sickness. You did that."

"I didn't know."

Pavel started forward, rubbed his casts together. "I telling nurses you are hurt her." A child shouted from down the hall.

"That isn't true," Tee said loudly. He tried to remember that he was taller than Pavel. "She told them I was her husband. She doesn't want you here."

Tee remembered the intensity that seemed to draw the artist's outer reaches in toward a central point, as Pavel's jaw clenched. There was a strange sense of déjà vu. The room breathed all at once, sucking in air.

"You say your father hurting people," Pavel muttered. "Who is hurting people really? You should watching out." His casts stiffened at his sides, and he stomped out to smoke.

Tee shook. He straightened his back, suddenly aware of his posture. At least it had been quick. He wanted to cry, but he wouldn't let Pavel hurt him. And then Rockefeller walked in—of course. Tee dared the two of them to do something. Blood rushed to his defense, to his head, his fists. He held on to his anger and righteousness.

"You didn't leaving Karlín," Rockefeller said. "Even after warning?"

"Sure," Tee said, "it's my fault. He hates me, I guess. But Katka doesn't." Like at the desk, though, his certainty left him. "What did they say? Is she going to be all right?"

Rockefeller shook his head.

The nurses craned to see the Asian against the giant Czech. "Forget her," Rockefeller said. Then he pinned Tee's arms, for a moment, before letting go with a grunt. Tee's biceps tingled. The strength in those fingers. "You are only kid."

White light shone off the walls and there was the cutting scent of bleach. Tee bit back tears. Rockefeller ran his hand through his bird-nest hair. Neither of them budged—until the doctor came in and said Katka was asking for Tee.

|||

Katka's doctor shuffled from side to side and said that the operation had at first seemed successful, but in fact the bacteria had already spread. He'd cut away as much infected tissue as possible. Now her organs had become a problem. Her liver and kidneys were shutting down. He continued in medical terms that hung in the air uninterpreted once he left. Tee wondered if the poor bedside manner was busyness or Katka's translation.

He stood on one side of her bed, Pavel on the other, Rockefeller in the corner behind the artist.

The wound was open to the air, since the gauze would have stuck to it. The debridement had sliced her calf down to a thin layer of muscle around her fibula. Her knee above looked like the head on a stick doll. She said the doctors didn't think cutting off her leg would help. The bacteria were in her bloodstream and her body couldn't handle the stress of an amputation. The bacteria ate away a lattice of flesh all the way up to her thigh, exposing muscle wrinkled like cauliflower. Pavel covered his mouth. Tee choked. Sweat beaded on Katka's face with each breath.

Tee wanted her to explain. She'd only had a scratch, a tiny cut closed with six stitches. He'd rushed her to the hospital twice where the doctors should have easily healed her.

Pavel wiped a tear with his shoulder. Behind him, Rockefeller shifted in place as if to warm up for a sport. It was a small room, but at least she had it to herself. She sat up slowly.

"I will explain everything," she said in English. "It is not your fault, Tee."

She switched to Czech, though Pavel said he could understand. As she talked, Pavel's eyes became thin lines. Tee imagined what she said. She didn't love Pavel, she'd made her choice with a clear mind. She would be fine. He should leave. She and Tee were going to tend a garden, buy a pet, far away.

But as she went on, her blue eyes clouding with a half-visible gray, Tee imagined she was telling Pavel she regretted leaving him. She'd made a mistake.

Tee should have learned more Czech. "You're going to be okay," he said. Her sharp cheekbones were sharper, the skin caved in. Her hands inched up her stomach. When her nails clicked together, he felt for the second time that day a sense of déjà vu. Her brown hair flowed neatly off the back of the pillow—she'd been able to think of this detail, to remember how she looked.

She exhaled a long breath, and at the end of it, she said, "Yes. I am going to be okay. But if I am not, I do not want any of you hating each other."

Tee could feel Pavel concentrating on translation.

"Do something for me," she said as electrical sounds echoed somewhere.

She shut her eyes for a moment. The smell of her leg burned in Tee's nose, itched his throat. She gestured Tee closer. Pavel turned and grunted from his chest. When Tee's ear was above her mouth, she whispered: "I want you to have that life."

"Which life?" he asked. He wished she would bite him. He lowered his ear.

"It is time to pretend."

Pavel clinked his casts on the metal rail. "I love you," he said in English, maybe so Tee would understand as well, so Tee would feel jealous, which he did, at how natural the interruption seemed. Husband to wife. Rockefeller stepped around the bed. One big hand fell on Tee's shoulder. Tee shrugged it off.

"Come," she said then. "All of you." As if they were her three children.

"Stop acting like you're eighty and have cancer," Tee said.

He held her hand. She brought his palm to Pavel's fingertips, which stuck out of the cast. The cold rough plaster. Holding them together with one hand, she reached her other for Rockefeller. Pavel grimaced. Tee heard a faint swallowing sound. Katka's shivers traveled into her wet hands. The room was silent and bright, too bright, and Pavel pulled his cast away and pounded the call button.

A nurse entered and waved them out. Tee wished he could have hit that button for Katka. She needed to rest and prepare for another surgery.

Rockefeller squeezed her hand and exited. Tee wanted to kiss her good-bye. He glanced down at her white, dying leg, so dull and detached from her red mouth, her blue eyes, her brown hair flowing off the back of the pillow. Pavel glared, his hair a snarl of lighter brown, waiting to be the last inside. Tee bent over her—but she shook her head.

He stopped inches from her face. He smelled the acrid wound. He didn't want to give Pavel a private good-bye. The nurse pressed his back, her hand disembodied, like it had come out of thin air. Katka smiled, a new wrinkle in the corner of her left eye.

"He can stay, Tee," she said. "They let family stay."

IV

Rockefeller said he had something Tee needed to see, so Tee agreed to stop at The Heavenly Café on the way to the house in Malešice. Tee couldn't think straight, his thoughts on Pavel alone with Katka, on her ruined leg.

The mall was about to close. They climbed the dead escalator to the second floor, and Rockefeller took a key from a cord around his neck and opened the café. It was clear why Tee was there. A mural covered the back wall, painted by Pavel's casts.

At first Tee couldn't tell what caused the pressure in the back of his head. The casts had made thick bands of yellow and blue and green. Wide black borders outlined everything like comic-book characters. The curves of Katka's body had become the curves of rushing water. Pavel had painted the flood. The debris in the water looked like the debris of the café. A swimmer rested in the bottom-left corner, emitting rays like an underwater sun. It seemed innocent enough, but Tee's container slowly filled.

Rockefeller said nothing. Tee kept staring until the swimmer, or the urgency with which Rockefeller had led him there, or the timing—after leaving Katka in the hospital—struck him with terrifying clarity.

He rubbed the back of his neck. "That's me, isn't it? Pavel painted me at the bottom of the flood."

Rockefeller moved around beside the mural. He was still taller than the painted body in the corner. Tee's body.

"Why are you showing me this?"

Rockefeller said the artist had asked him to make this happen. He played with his lapel. "If I am hurting you," he said, "then Pavel will forgive me."

The resignation in those eyes was like two immovable rocks. "You would do it?" Tee said. He backed away. "What now? Should I call the police? The embassy?"

"So now you leave from Prague." Rockefeller crossed over the slabs of concrete. His corduroy jacket clung too tightly to his wide shoulders, as if it was concealing wings. Here, Tee thought, in The Heavenly Café, was the Angel of Death. He wished to make a joke.

"She's dying soon," Rockefeller whispered when he was even with Tee. "You cannot staying here."

Tee planted his leg. "She's not dying." He remembered his father's call in September, to say that his uncle had died, the buzz of finality. Tee didn't feel that now. He forced himself to memorize the mural, and he remembered his palms: an early death or a coma. In his apartment, Katka had taken one look at the molten pewter, and cried. "How could you say that?"

"You have to go before she goes," Rockefeller said.

They went to Pavel and Katka's house to sleep, unable to return to Karlín. Tee took the bed. He wanted Rockefeller to know he wasn't running away. Rockefeller said nothing. He'd been silent since the café. When Tee stripped down for a shower, he saw that his father had called again, sometime since the hospital. He hadn't felt the vibration.

He stepped into the shower Pavel and Katka had used for a dozen years, at times surely together. As the clean water washed off the smell and grime of the flood, he imagined them in the hospital. Pavel glowing that she had rejected Tee's kiss, Katka's palm clammy on his bicep. Maybe Pavel expected Tee, at that very moment, to be drowning. To his wife, Pavel apologized. He had never purposefully hurt her, though that didn't make it any better. He would suck the poison from her leg if he could. She was sorry, too. She said Tee had caused the infection. Tee hadn't listened.

Pavel and Katka would fall into their old rhythm: painting, posing. She would say, *your art, your art*; and he would say, *Jára Cimrman will always be our hero*; and they would share that secret laugh.

When Tee was dressed in the clothes from his plastic bags, he found himself standing beside the back of the giant canvas. He turned it around. Katka's yellow ripples. That painting seemed the opposite of the mural in the café: her bright immortality, his dark drowning. Then he remembered the other painting Pavel had done. He searched the room, and then the closet, but he couldn't find it. In the closet, he looked through the door ready for the ghost. If it was ever there. A wind shook the curtains, and he noticed one window was cracked.

When Tee went to bed, Rockefeller was still pacing the living room. Tee set his phone alarm for five A.M. and lay awake to the heavy footsteps.

In the end Pavel's friendship had been worth more to Rockefeller than money, and Tee didn't want to bribe anyone ever again. If Katka died, Rockefeller would attack Tee—that was the deal? And when Katka recovered? What then?

Tee wondered if his uncle, or his mother, had ever plotted revenge. Maybe his uncle had planned to crash his plane with his father in it. Maybe his mother had planned to run away and start a new family. He imagined his mother tracing a finger over his father's nose, late at night, then over her adopted son's. The same shape. On another night, she compared the noses with a ruler. She snipped locks of their hairs. But no, she said she didn't have proof.

His father must have met his birth mother on one of the two initial visits, before he took the job. He was walking absentmindedly, comparing Korea to a film about Korea that he had watched before he left, when a skinny woman broke away from her friends. She wanted to practice her English, or she was curious about foreigners. Her tongue flicked to the three dots at the corner of her mouth, and he invited her to the hotel he was going to work for. He handed her a business card, making up his mind in that instant.

Tee felt the need to call his father, picturing that obsessive gaze, those hangdog cheeks. He weighed his cell in his hand. Rockefeller was still moving around on the other side of the wall. His father's number glowed in the dark room. They hadn't spoken since Tee's trip back to Boston, since his father's trip to California. The thought crossed Tee's mind, though he pushed it away, that his father could offer advice. How to be with a married woman, how to stave off the backlash, emotional and physical. Or at least how to accept it. Tee thumbed the call button.

As if his thumb had reached out, the screen flashed. He listened to the ring. He felt his throat closing, a fist for an Adam's apple. When he hung up, he could breathe again.

In Tee's dreams, Pavel and Rockefeller pushed his face into the fissure in Katka's leg. He could smell the sewage in her cut, the festering bacteria; he could see the disease chomping after her cells. Slowly they tipped up his feet, and he slid inside. He tried to swim away through her blood, but the mouths of the disease followed him, biting at his heels. Finally he realized he was asleep, and he tore himself out of the dream, though the feeling that he was inside her remained. In his daze, he could make out a tall figure beside the bed. The moon was trapped behind rain clouds, and the room was almost black. Then he knew who it was. He didn't know if Rockefeller could see him, too, see that he was awake. The giant body seemed like only a collection of shadows. Neither of them breathed. Then Tee whispered, "Rock?" and the shadows slowly receded.

V

Tee and Rockefeller got to the hospital first thing in the morning, after a silent cab ride. The smell in Katka's room, forgotten by a shower and a night's sleep, sent Tee into a coughing fit.

Pavel stood on one side of the bed. A woman Tee didn't recognize stood on the other. Katka lay between them, grinding her teeth. The IV dripped into her veins and machines beeped loudly. Pus stained the sheets around the wound.

Tee stood on the woman's side, not next to Pavel. Rockefeller stood on Pavel's side, near the door. The woman extended her hand to Tee. "I am Kateřina's mother," she said. All at once he saw Katka's high cheekbones and blue eyes. Her mother spoke English well, though in a clipped manner, as if still addressing her abusive British husband.

Pavel must have called her. Tee noticed Katka's discomfort. He shook her mother's hand and asked if the doctor had been in to say when Katka could leave.

"Who are you, then?" her mother asked Tee. "You are from China?"

"A friend," Tee said, telling himself not to react. Pavel grunted, but added nothing.

"The doctor said she is lucky to survive night and still talk now," her mother said.

Finally Katka spoke rapidly in Czech, then seemed to lose her train of thought, then started again. The strange gray from the day before filmed over her irises. Her hair still hung off the back of the pillow. Had she put it up again or had she not moved all night? Tee wished she would give an excuse for why she hadn't kissed him the day before. What she did say equally thrilled him.

Pavel banged his casts on the railing of the bed, and Katka reached across her mother for Tee's hand and said, "He is my American lover," in English.

Tee remembered how she had pulled him away from the Thai massage parrot in Old Town. She was always giving him his self back. She mumbled something else, which Tee couldn't understand, and her mother made a little hiccup of surprise. Rockefeller mumbled in Czech and left the room.

"Just because you never took a lover, Mum," Katka said, "does not mean I should not." Pavel banged his casts on the rail again.

Katka's mother rested her hand by her daughter's neck and said something in Czech that didn't sound like disagreement, and Katka's grip tightened on Tee's fingers. Her skin was wet and cold. He rubbed her hands warm. Pavel rocked on his heels, and then he was waving his casts around. He shouted in Czech, and her mother stroked her head, perhaps comparing her son-in-law to her late husband. Small split-open mounds stuck out from Katka's infected thigh like rotten peaches half-buried in her skin.

Katka waited for Pavel to finish. Then she shouted back, her face ghosting away its color. Footsteps rushed down the hall, and Pavel cried. Only a day had passed since Katka was a calm peacemaker, holding their hands together.

At last she lowered her voice. Her mother went to intercept the nurse. Pavel scratched his casts against his pants. He moved for her hand, and she brushed him away. She muttered relentlessly, until he rubbed his eyes with his shoulder and stepped outside.

Katka's mother looked back at Tee from the doorway and said, "I can see she must love you, but I hope you did not do any what her husband says."

"It's all my fault," Tee said.

She smiled as if she didn't understand him, and followed Pavel into the hall.

When they were alone, Katka's voice broke down and she said hoarsely, "I cannot concentrate." She closed her eyes and seemed to disappear for a moment. Her cheeks trembled, the loose skin of a balloon. When she returned to him, she was old, far older than their fifteen-year gap. He saw again the new wrinkle at the corner of her eye, and he could hear the snap of teeth as the disease swam beneath her surface, like in his dream. His fingers went to her cords absentmindedly.

"I am going to die soon," she said, her voice getting stronger again. "I know you do not want to hear that, but I am going to die soon. Do you understand?"

His vision blurred, and he held the railing so he wouldn't fall.

"I knew all along," she said, "you were going to be the end of Pavel and me. I only thought it would be sooner."

As his eyes refocused, death was present at last. He remembered her on the stairs behind him as they tried to get on the roof, the mismatched sounds of her steps, he realized now. *You will keep me safe*, she had said. She had trusted him.

"I do not know why I cannot forgive you," she whispered. She seemed to push her breath out with her voice. "In the end we were going to be with each other with or without a flood. You should have let us leave."

He wanted to throw up. She had waited until he couldn't respond, and now, after she said she was going to die, she accused him.

For an instant, surrounded by the beeping of her machines, he wished they had never been together. He wanted her to be with Pavel. He wanted to say it was her fault—that first time, she had kissed him and he had refused. He wanted her to live forever, without him. He wanted to say he didn't need her to accuse him. He wanted to hate her because she was alive somewhere, and he couldn't go to her, not hate her because she was dead.

She muttered in Czech. He wouldn't realize until later that she was saying she loved him. "Let me say good-bye to my husband," she added in English.

Tee wanted to stay. But he knew he had to do this—for her, and even for Pavel.

In the hallway he said, "She wants to talk to you," and lowered his head as if she'd chosen her husband in the end. Rockefeller walked back with three cups of coffee. Pavel took one and went in. Tee sank to the tile beside Katka's mother and cried. She waited for him to speak, but a piece of glass was lodged in his voice box and would cut into it at a single word. Inside of him, his organs squeezed like a fist. His chest shuddered.

Finally he forced himself to say something. "It is my fault," he whispered.

Katka's mother sucked in her breath and said, "It is never fault of who claims it." But Tee crossed to the other side of the hall. He couldn't look at her. He had killed her daughter.

A dozen sobs later, Pavel shouted for help. Katka had slipped into a coma.

VI

The doctor gave Katka four days. Tee returned to the hospital each morning and slept in the bed in Malešice each night, while Pavel stayed by her side. Rockefeller gave Tee the same four days. Tee had hoped that Katka's last words would appease Pavel; of course, they did not. Maybe the coma foretold in Tee's palms was Katka's. As the floodwater drained, it revealed billions of dollars of damage, eleven people dead, hundreds of thousands homeless, buildings that had survived wars now in danger. A chemical plant had leaked chlorine gas that caused scratchy throats, as if the city had caught a cold. Karlín was still off-limits.

In Katka's hospital room, Pavel glared without talking. Katka's mother cried tears saved up over a decade of regret. In the house in Malešice, the mural haunted Tee's dreams. He woke sweating and looking for Rockefeller's shadow. Rockefeller never seemed to sleep. Tee lay awake in Katka's bed until early morning. He had carried through the flood two notebooks, some clothes, and his cell phone in a plastic bag, while she carried her disease. He turned off his cell, turned off the outside world, tried to turn off the fluttering inside him.

The first day of the coma, he felt as if invisible strings hung in the air, wires of life, and if he tripped the right one, she would sit up. He waved his arms above her and ignored Pavel and Rockefeller.

The second day, he waited until Pavel went to the bathroom, and then he bent in and kissed her. Her mother patted his back, or weakly struck him.

The third day, he held Katka's hand and told her everything he could think of, not caring how stupid it sounded, from his first memory—flying in his uncle's plane—to the last thing he did before coming to Prague—praying, embarrassedly, with his mother, both of them wanting new lives. He told her he wished he'd been able to talk to his uncle, not just to try to change his mind, but to tell him he had meant something important, at least to Tee. Pavel grumbled, at first, but eventually gave up, later speaking to Rockefeller in the hall. Her mother tugged at her sleeves and whispered her own good-byes.

Tee found himself staring longingly at Katka's hands, hands that had explored every inch of his body. Those rainy days, she'd seen him exposed—like the inside of a flower as the petals peel away. Now her fingers seemed the phantoms of those petals, the history of his exposure in her skin. He couldn't lose her. He couldn't stand to go back to before her touch.

The third day, he murmured her name again and again, for a moment forgetting when he'd done the same with his birth mother's name, in the woods. For a moment Katka was the only Katka there. No distortions in the closet, no ghosts.

The third day of the coma, as he and Rockefeller left the hospital, Rockefeller said, "So what are you deciding?" Tee wanted to be hurt. He suggested they go for a beer. He remembered the night he'd invited Pavel and Rockefeller for drinks, with Ynez.

They went to one of the randomly numbered pubs around the city, and Tee drank quickly, tipping back Krušovice, trying to drown out all the possible harm—his head still somehow seemed more frightening than reality. They sat next to the window, and endless strangers passed by, refugees of the flood. Their dull bodies warmed under the light of streetlamps.

"What was the Revolution like?" Tee asked after the first beer.

"I knew that once," Rockefeller said, bags under his eyes. "But now is different. Once, when Pavel saying we did nothing, we not causing Revolution, I did not believe him."

"Now, what, you believe in fate?"

"I am believing freedom comes in end, but each of us aren't free."

They were silent for a minute, and Tee recalled that first evening he and Katka rushed up to his apartment in the rain, the inevitability. "You don't have to do this," he said.

He went for another beer. At the bar he thought about slipping out and finding a hotel that still had vacancies. How far would he have to go? He spun the coaster on the counter. When he looked up, Rockefeller was there.

"I have to," Rockefeller said. "Please leave."

Tee couldn't let Katka die without him, though—even his father had claimed that right of his birth mother. Rockefeller ordered a slivovice. Tee's breaths shortened. He sucked through the foam on his beer.

When Tee said there was a choice, Rockefeller said, "I chosen Pavel."

With the third beer, Tee realized Rockefeller's resolve was never going to soften. Tension rolled like a ball, hard and smooth, through his shoulders. "Let's get out of here," he said. "I have to do something before the end." Rockefeller thudded his empty glass on the table and sighed. As they left the bar, Tee heard a man say one of the seals from the zoo had managed to swim to Western Europe. But once there, it had died of exhaustion.

They walked through Vinohrady into New Town, nursing a bottle of Becherovka they bought at a convenience store. Rockefeller trailed slightly behind, as if he might attack at any moment. Tee wanted to ask for a little longer, at least, but he didn't dare. The sun set quickly. The alcohol tasted like pine trees. "Christmasy," he said, recalling the drink from New Year's.

Rockefeller's shadow would sometimes stretch from a streetlamp and engulf Tee's. Six and a half feet.

By the time they reached Wenceslas Square, they'd both "pulled an elephant," as the Czech saying went. The lights spun. They stood beside the National Museum with the wide legs of the Elysées-like boulevard below them. People still went to clubs, still talked in the streets, still made plans for tomorrows. Tee stood before a monument to the protesters who'd burned themselves. "You think they got what they wanted?" he asked. He wished to empty his container for good, return everything he'd taken, set the past on fire.

"Where we are going?" Rockefeller said. "Dark is coming soon." He stumbled a little. He thumped his hand on Tee's back to catch himself.

Tee stumbled, too, and turned quickly. But Rockefeller was wiping his face. Tee pretended he hadn't forgotten to breathe. He took the bottle from Rockefeller and said he could still smell the flood.

The roads wound them into Old Town, where the fireworks had whizzed over his half-naked body and a beautiful woman had waved at him. In the square, couples sat on the benches around the statue of Jan Hus, who'd been burned at the stake as a heretic. Prague turned villains into heroes, and vice versa. "Pavel told me a joke about the presidential flag once," Tee said. The slogan on the flag translated to "Truth will win," but without one accent mark, it would be "Truth belongs to the winner."

"Why you are staying here?" Rockefeller said, taking back the bottle.

"You were my friend," Tee said. Was.

When they came to the front of the Rudolfinum, Tee turned left along the river. He kept feeling objects hurtling at his back. He resisted the urge to duck. He pictured Katka in the nothingness of her coma, searching for a way out. Did she hear him and her mother and Pavel and Rockefeller outside?

Rockefeller muttered loudly to himself. The sky was dark and the streetlamps seemed to get brighter and brighter. The scent of sewage and cleaning missions clung to the air. Tee coughed, his throat sore with chlorine. If only the river had been chlorinated earlier. Ahead was the Charles Bridge. The swollen Vltava roared. Several mechanical cranes perched on the bridge. One of them dipped into the river and fished out a tree trunk, and someone clapped.

Tee walked under the Old Town bridge tower and over the water. Both sides of the bridge were lined with statues. He recognized St. Jan of Nepomuk by the oiled bronze of the plaque, well worn by superstitious hands, by the drawing Katka had done for him during the flood. Rockefeller tipped back the Becherovka, and Tee ran to rub the saint who promised to return him to Prague. When he reached the statue, though, he wanted more than a return. He felt the smooth plaque under his hand. The river swept below. He pulled himself up as if Katka was still in her tree above and Rockefeller still at the bottom.

"What you are doing?" Rockefeller said. "You are tourist after all."

Tee heard the murmur of bystanders. He balanced on the lower tier of the statue and tried to reach higher, away from the chorus. "You touch him and you always come back. He's the saint of swimmers."

"Is only legend," Rockefeller said. "And is not to climb." He tugged Tee's pant leg. He said the Church had de-sainted Jan. The tongue from the Vltava had only been a piece of brain, maybe not related, and the murder had been political.

"That can't be true," Tee said, but Rockefeller had no reason to lie. The hair at the peak of Rockefeller's head was starting to fall out and it stuck up as if he were too tall even for mirrors. One big hand wrapped around Tee's ankle. The throng on the bridge clamored. "Now," Tee said. "Do it now. Drown me."

The water below was dark and loud. Rockefeller's other hand clasped Tee's back. Tee imagined haunting the river after his death, calling people back to Prague. He sucked in air and prepared for eternal swimming. But Rockefeller was pulling him down, not pushing him over. Tee tried for a second longer to cling to the statue, to stay up, to start to fall. Rockefeller was too strong.

On the bridge Tee steadied himself, then walked quickly away as he heard cheers. They thought he had been rescued. He snatched the bottle off of the wall, where Rockefeller had left it, steadied himself again, and took a long pull. Rockefeller followed and drank with him.

Tee slumped onto one of the benches and wept.

CHAPTER 7
HOMECOMINGS

I

In Boston, in the rehabilitation center, Tee would try to figure out what had happened to him. From an article in the *Prague Post*, he learned that Rockefeller was in jail—described as "a former proponent of the Velvet Revolution whose parents are suspected Communists." Pavel's new series of paintings made its way to New York, but Tee didn't care to see the "groundbreaking" works.

As his balance improved, he was cleared for a day out. His parents took him to the Cape for the afternoon, as they used to do when he was little. He walked along the beach and remembered colliding with a random white kid as they both ran for a seagull. The boy had started to cry, and the boy's father had come up and demanded to know where Tee's parents were. Tee had pointed at his parents at the top of the beach, but the man hadn't believed him. The man had scanned the crowd, and then had seemed suddenly to pity Tee. He had shouted for his son to follow, and had turned away. The boy called Tee a Chink as he took off. Tee had made his way back to his parents and had asked them why the man didn't believe him. His parents could have told him then, perhaps, about his birth mother, but his father had given the old sticks and stones line instead.

What had that pity been? Had the man recognized the similarity between his father and him, and seen no mother? Or was their skin color enough that the man couldn't see the similarity at all?

A conch shell glinted on the beach, and Tee reached for it and toppled into the water. His mother rushed in and pulled him out. She said the Cape might not have been the best idea.

Back in the rehab center, Tee sat in the library and tried to hear the twanging he'd heard before, to call the ghost woman to him with his imagination. The door opened. It was the man with the old war wound. When the man asked what he was doing, Tee decided to tell him the truth. The man said he often saw people. He'd even learned to accept it when they shot at him, to imagine the bullets passed right through, though really, they lodged in his guts and jiggled like coins as he walked. And then, as if that had conjured her, the woman glowed past the door, her nose small and her cheeks like a short cliff dropping down to the pool of her mouth. Tee thanked the man, and ran after her. "Katka," he called, but as his voice trembled and his legs held steady for once, he knew it wasn't her.

That night on the Charles Bridge, the last moments Tee could remember in Prague, he had cried on the bench and Rockefeller had rested a hand on his shoulder. Then Tee had either blacked out, or the force of the impact had blacked him out. He remembered Rockefeller's hand, flashes of a Czech hospital, not the one Katka was in, his father's ear against his chest, the long flight home. He imagined what Rockefeller had been thinking. At some point Rockefeller had understood that his promise could not be undone. Maybe as they drank too much and pitied themselves, Tee said that Rockefeller was a fraud, never a friend to Pavel or him or anyone. Or maybe Pavel called and asked if it was over, or called about Katka. Rockefeller swigged the Becherovka, and as he brought his hand down, he saw how easy it could be, and he surprised himself by cracking the bottle over the back of Tee's head.

Once Tee lay still, Rockefeller remembered the graveyard. Now he was the attacker, the Americans. He poured the rest of the alcohol on Tee's face to wake him. He shook Tee before noticing the slack neck, the head rattling. He was unable to take it back. He searched for Tee's cell. When he turned it on, missed calls flashed by. He pressed the call button over the first person on the list, the last person Tee had called, his father, and said Tee was hurt, badly, without explaining why or how.

Then he called emergency. Or did he call emergency first, even before thinking through the consequences? That when they saw the body, they would know what he'd done. They knew bodies, the language of bruises and cuts and attempted murder. The doctor would know, as soon as they got to the hospital. Rockefeller might have to tell them himself, to give Tee the best shot of waking quickly. Rockefeller pictured the café never finished, but even if he was the type of person who could attack Tee, he couldn't leave Tee in the aftermath.

The ambulance arrived, and the paramedics lifted Tee onto the stretcher, as Katka had been lifted. The moon yawned through the clouds for an instant and disappeared again. Rockefeller got into the front seat, feeling sorry for himself. Maybe on the way, the medics recognized the signs of an assault and called the police. When the ambulance arrived at the hospital, a squad car waited. Rockefeller gave up then, or thought that if he accepted his punishment, he wouldn't be such a monster. Or he even tried to tell them he had found Tee like this. Maybe he took responsibility only at the last moment, since Pavel would not be satisfied if the injury was an accident.

Rockefeller gave his statement, not fumbling his words, not blaming Pavel, and the policemen guided him to the car. He turned and bowed his head, and they slapped the cuffs on him. They might even have said he did the noble thing, taking Tee to the hospital instead of running away. He needed to hear this: he needed to know he wasn't the Secret Police of his youth, as he had always carried the guilt of his parents' politics and the guilt of sending them away. He had always wanted forgiveness even more than freedom.

Tee's father hopped the first flight out. He arrived in Prague in the morning and filed charges before taking his son home.

In the rehab center, Tee wrote and wrote. Sometimes he would imagine a library fished from the flood, ruined books that only had meaning for the people who'd lost them. He would try to rewrite the stories he'd scribbled in the margins of those novels from the Globe, but he would grow so tired trying to remember that he would fall asleep with the typewriter on his lap. He would leave memory behind for dreams. The pages he wrote turned increasingly to his father in Korea. The sun and the sand and the spa. His father waiting for his birth mother to appear at lunch and lift his hand to her belly. When she started showing, had his father denied Tee was his? His father was always a coward. Yet Tee had reason to believe his birth mother had made his father brave. His father had brought Tee back to Boston, saving a Polaroid of her for her son. He had kept her image beside him, as present in Tee's face as a never-ending film, as a story told and retold.

II

In the rehabilitation center, Tee took care to protect his head, to rest if he felt tired. Time was less like a locked house. He remembered what day it was, and that days passed in a line. For the most part, his parents, too, seemed to let time pass. They had quit complaining about each other, whether for his sake or their own. His aunt, his father said, was getting genuine psychiatric help. Tee was learning not to draw attention to his psychoses. He could make his past appear before him, but at least his visions never spoke, or hurt anyone.

The Monday the rehab center finally released him, his parents took him to dinner. He suggested the fortune-telling restaurant in Chinatown, only it had gone out of business. They ended up down the street at a Thai place. They sat under a mounted sailfish and discussed Tee's future. He would stay with his mother until the house sold. His father had bought an apartment in Somerville. His mother had her new job and exercise program and even new habits—she rolled her shoulders now, whenever Tee said something that gave her pause. His father had finally given up on Hollywood. Tee would go back to school next fall. As they told him how much they loved him, he wondered where all the desperation of the past year had gone, as if he were the only one who recalled the film and the divorce and Prague. His father cupped Tee's cheek like a puppy's. His mother brought out a cake and lit candles. Tee's container filled—for a moment, he couldn't tell where he was. He saw the shadows on Katka's face as she was dying, or in the darkness of the flood, or perhaps in a dream, and he remembered the feeling just before he fell out of her tree, that she had something more to say.

Back in his childhood home, Tee found *The Giving Tree* on a bookshelf in his mother's bedroom. She still had her favorite children's books there, ones they had shared when Tee was a boy. His mother, Katka's father. What was it about this tree that made it a parental favorite? Katka had given Tee everything—her apples, her branches, her trunk—in only a few short months. He missed her with a cinching pain in his lungs.

At the end of the story, the boy the tree loves is an old man, and the tree is a stump. The man uses up everything, both the tree and himself, on a life the reader never sees. Tee put the book back on its shelf. In his bedroom, he stapled a line of yarn to the floor to keep practicing his balance. Online, he would find a list of symptoms common to head trauma: poor memory, poor attention to detail, poor decision-making, impulsiveness, disorientation, language problems, inability to understand when spoken to. How many of these symptoms had already been his before the flood?

Each time Tee went over to his father's apartment, he wondered if he might find the walls covered in drawings again. But somehow his father had figured out how to stop his fixations. His father would ask what Tee was writing—and Tee admitted that he was writing fiction, that he had to change his story to have any hope of figuring out what it was.

It was the Sunday after his release, Tee would remember, that his father dropped two manila folders on the coffee table between them. Tee felt something about to float through the door. In the first folder was a thick stack of paper. "Thank you for letting me read your stories," his father said. "But I want to know the truth. Can you tell me what really happened to you in Prague?"

Tee said as far as he knew, he'd gotten a head wound and ended up back in Boston.

"I've been receiving something in the mail," his father said after a moment. In the second folder were two envelopes addressed from Prague.

Immediately Tee could smell rain. He asked what was in the envelopes, who had sent them. Then he took a deep breath. "Katka," he said mostly to himself, "is dead."

His father raised an eyebrow. "They're letters from the guy who did this to you. Rockefeller. His English isn't great. I was going to wait to show them to you, but your mom didn't want me to hide anything."

"Is Katka dead?" Tee asked.

"You'd better look for yourself."

Tee fingered the slits from the letter opener. The envelopes were addressed to his father. How had Rockefeller found the address? Pavel must have found it on the Internet.

Tee opened the first letter and read slowly. Rockefeller apologized. *Can I saying sorry?* he wrote. *I was too much into my head. I didn't see I was doing wrong.* He thanked Tee's father for flying on short notice. In the first letter, Katka was still alive, still in her coma, fighting the bacteria. Tee started planning to return. In the second letter, she slipped away. Rockefeller said Pavel was painting her one final time, and despite their anger, Tee should see the painting; Pavel and Tee should forgive each other. The letter was dated eight days earlier.

"Are you okay?" his father asked.

Tee sensed the ghost woman nearby. Rockefeller still didn't understand what he had done to Tee; Pavel still believed art had gained and lost him a wife. Tee was a person who couldn't remember his favorite songs. Without Katka, there was no Prague to return to, no magic in the statue of Jan of Nepomuk. Tee was still in the middle of the flood. He realized he had loved Katka most truly when he wanted Rockefeller to hurt him. He thought about what the man with the old war wound had said—about the bullets jingling inside his body—just before the ghost appeared and the three freckles on the woman came clear. Tee remembered holding his birth mother's photograph above him, lying in bed, bringing that face down close to his and then away.

"Dad," he said. "I need to know about her."

His father tapped the letters and frowned. "I only know what's written there."

"No," Tee said. "I don't mean Katka. I know Katka. Tell me about my birth mother."

Finally the room rustled with presence. Tee steadied himself—the flood washed through, and he had nothing to hold on to except for a ghost—and then she was there. He was standing beside his father, and he was standing beside his birth mother. The bird in his throat took flight. He said he knew about the affair, and the truth about his birth. What he didn't know about was her, the woman he'd come from. All his life, he'd either clung to an empty Korea, or he'd filled it with myths.

His father stood and mixed a drink. "Whatever I say won't be enough," he warned.

"Tell me," Tee said again and again, late into the night.

ACKNOWLEDGMENTS

Over the decade it took to write this book, I met my wife, became a father, moved at least a dozen times. I am thankful to so many people and places. I have tried to capture a certain idea of Prague, and to that end, I have taken some liberties. For example, the bookstore Tee works in takes its name from a bookstore in Prague, though the physical details differ. The characteristics of Tee's Globe come from my head.

It is amazing to work with an Asian American editor on an Asian American novel. Thank you to Vivian Lee. Also to Tara Parsons, Al Woodworth, and the rest of Little A. Thank you to Chelsea Lindman, who keeps the faith. Thank you to Patrick Barry for the beautiful cover.

Thanks most of all to my family—to my parents and siblings and especially to Ok Kyung Na, who (in so many ways) is the reason I was able to write this book, and to my daughter, who is the reason I was able to understand it. Thank you, wherever she is, to my birth mother.

Thank you to everyone who read earlier drafts, especially to Margot Livesey, whose wisdom and generosity are a light; to Mako Yoshikawa's novel-class crew (Katharine Gingrich and Dan Pribble in particular); to Robert Boswell, whose advice guided me through the last stages of revision; to Kirstin Chen, who always reassures me; and to Cathy Chung, Roxane Gay, Laura van den Berg, Alyssa Knickerbocker, Carmie Banasky, James Scott, Ken Calhoun, and Amanda O'Brien.

Thank you to Asmin Tulpule for the medical advice.

I am curiously indebted to a passing remark by Mat Johnson. I am indebted to my EFL students from when I lived in Prague, who told me many of these myths and superstitions in service of their English, and to my old flatmates. I also consulted several guidebooks and several books of myth that I have since, sadly, misplaced. The Internet helped immensely.

Thank-yous to: Emerson College, the *Good Men Project*, the Wiener Center, the Bonchon crew, Grub Street, the Bread Loaf Writers' Conference, the Fourth Kingdom (especially Alex Chee and Don Lee), the adoptee and APIA communities, the University of Houston, Inprint, Putney (and Henk Rossouw), Michael Seidlinger, Deena Drewis, Mink Choi, and all the editors and writers and friends who have done so much. You are too many to name. I am grateful for that. I am grateful for you.

It's been a long journey, but in the end, I touched the statue of Jan of Nepomuk twice, once on either side of a decade. A great writer once said, you end the story where you see it starting to return.

Thank you for reading.

ABOUT THE AUTHOR

Photo © 2011 Stephanie Mitchell

Matthew Salesses was adopted from Korea at age two. He has written about adoption and race for NPR's *Code Switch*, the *New York Times Motherlode* blog, and *Salon*, and his fiction has appeared in *Guernica/PEN*, *Glimmer Train*, and *American Short Fiction*, among others. He is the fiction editor and a contributing writer at the *Good Men Project*. He is also the author of *I'm Not Saying, I'm Just Saying*. *The Hundred-Year Flood* is his first full-length novel.